The 7th Dimension

A NOVEL

MONICA BROUSSARD

FROM THE TINY ACORN . . .
GROWS THE MIGHTY OAK

www.AcornPublishingLLC.com

For information, address:
Acorn Publishing, LLC
3943 Irvine Blvd. Ste. 218
Irvine, CA 92602

The 7th Dimension

Edited by Kat Ross
Cover design by Damonza
Interior design and formatting by Debra Cranfield Kennedy

Printed in the United States of America

ISBN-13: 979-8-88528-102-7 (hardcover)
ISBN-13: 979-8-88528-099-0 (paperback)
Library of Congress Control Number: 2024906457

AUTHOR'S NOTE

To my readers: My writing highlights the significance of self-awareness and self-compassion in times of trauma.

With firsthand experience, I understand the overwhelming feelings and confusion that come with life-altering events.

Although it may seem counterintuitive, taking time for self-care practices such as meditation, prayer, and physical activity can strengthen one's ability to face future challenges.

I pray that my words will offer comfort and direction to others on their journey toward healing.

This book is dedicated to my family and friends whose love, support, and friendship have been my strength and inspiration. This book would not exist without you. I am forever grateful, and I hope this book justifies my love and appreciation for you all. Thank you for being a part of my life and making it much more prosperous. Here's to many more adventures and memories together.

Chapter 1

Derek Hollinger stood motionless, transfixed by his own sorrow and by the wood-grain pattern of his penthouse door. His fingertips moved along the ridges and dips as if they were a roadmap to some unknown kingdom. He was lost in this journey when suddenly, a thud from inside the elevator shaft jarred him back to the moment. He wasn't sure how long he had been standing there, but it felt like hours.

Three weeks had passed, and he was no closer to finding answers to why he had woken up one morning with his entire body covered in tattoos; he still had no clue what they meant or how to get rid of them.

The sound of the elevator motor humming in the vestibule seemed distant now. The world was blurring away. The longer he stared, the further he felt removed from reality.

With shoulders slumped, he forced himself to insert his key into the lock. He wasn't sure what he should be searching for, but he knew he had to hold onto the glimmer of hope that flickered in the depths of his mind. Eventually, he would find the answer.

Derek eased the door open and stepped into the spacious penthouse, dropping his bag at his feet. He took a deep breath, then paused to exhale and inspect the familiar surroundings. Now back in his own space, he allowed himself a moment to soak in the strong sensation of familiarity. The abandoned room served as a reminder of his not-so-distant past—a metaphor for his anguished feelings.

Despite the lavishness of the penthouse, there was a strange sense of stillness in the air, as if the room itself were holding its breath in anticipation of what was to come. The chairs, upholstered in a rich gray full-grain leather, sat empty. Their high backs arched toward one another like two lovers whose arms extended in an eternal embrace. They seemed to be waiting for two people to fill them, to complete the picture of symmetry and balance in the room.

Derek scanned the opulent furnishings and decor, a testament to the wealth and power of the apartment's owner. The walls were a deep historical shade of burgundy, representing ambition, wealth, and power, and in the center of the room, the floor was covered in a plush Persian carpet practically begging to be walked on barefoot.

Yet the room sat untouched—a showroom display. Shelves of unread books lined the far side of the room and looked as if they had been abandoned long ago.

He let out an audible deep sigh. As the front door closed, a sudden rush of nausea made his heart slam against his chest. He could feel the palpitations vibrate through his throat and neck. The past month had been traumatic and ecstatic at the same time, but this visceral reaction to his return home and the separation from Kendal caught him off guard. He wasn't sure exactly what they were to each other, but he'd come to depend on her—his port in the storm.

He wished Kendal had come with him. Instead, he found himself engulfed in a strange and intense loneliness. Feelings of helplessness and despair. The elation he'd felt living with Kendal in her tiny little apartment had evaporated. He desperately wanted to turn around and rush back to her.

Funny, how he'd hardly noticed her for all those years they worked together. Before his life fell apart, Derek was one of L.A.'s top plastic surgeons. Kendal had been his nurse and office manager. She was bright and competent, yet he'd taken her for granted until the fateful night when he was attending an awards dinner and had a bizarre encounter outside the hotel with an old woman, whom he now believed to be some kind of shaman.

Whatever she'd done to him—a curse?—he'd woken up after days of illness with grotesque tattoos covering every inch of his body. Only Kendal had been there for him in the aftermath, letting him stay at her place, covering for him with patients and the other doctors, and supporting him on the painful, surreal journey to learn the truth of what had happened to him.

Derek had fallen for her, and he knew she cared about him, too. But getting closer to Kendal had also exposed his deep-seated emotional issues, traumas that went back to childhood. He knew they could no longer be ignored. Strong feelings of worthlessness had crept into their relationship. He had found it increasingly difficult to communicate with her about the mysterious arrangement of tattoos now covering his body.

He would sometimes lash out when he felt agitated or restless. His tolerance had been low, his temper short, and everything and everyone got on his nerves. To make things more complicated, it was time to go back to work. Some of the tattoos had disappeared, but others were still scattered intermittently across his skin.

He reached down for his bag and continued to the master bedroom. The polished hardwood floors with natural stone accents swept past an unused massive kitchen with stainless steel appliances and quartz countertops. As he trudged slowly down the span of the hall to the master, he felt like a long-lost lover returning home and having to apologize for his absence.

He dropped the bag on the bedroom floor and sat down on his bed. The Jacuzzi he had used after those exhausting days of surgery sat empty on the outside balcony of the master bedroom. His solitary soaks now seemed like a distant dream. The wraparound terrace had very little furniture.

His bleak outlook was telling him that nothing would ever get better and there was nothing he could do to improve the situation. Tears of hopelessness ran down his face as he sat reflecting on the events that had played out in the past couple of weeks. The sound of his cellphone brought him back to the present.

Wiping his partially tattooed eyes, Derek got up and reached into his pocket. He cleared his throat as he looked at Kendal's smiling face on the wallpaper of his cellphone. "Hello?"

"Hey, you. How are you doing?" her cheery voice gushed from his phone.

"Not good." Her bright disposition felt nonsensical. "I feel lost without you."

"Now, that's what I like to hear," she joked.

"Kendal, I'm serious. I'm feeling really nervous. I don't know if I can go through with this." He paced back and forth, the stillness of the room suffocating him.

Kendal sighed. "Of course, you can. I know you're scared, but this is something that has to be done. But if you need me to come over, I will," she offered hesitantly.

"Yeah, I do—No, I don't. I don't know..." He rubbed his

forehead. "No, I don't think it would be fair to you. You already explained your feelings about the whole living together thing."

"Whoa … Wait a second, I didn't say anything about moving in. I meant that I could come over to keep you company for a while."

"Well, then, I guess I better just deal with this because if you come over here, there is no way I am going to let you leave."

"I'm glad you warned me before I made that mistake," she teased.

"I'll see you in the office tomorrow." Derek started to hang up.

"Wait, wait. Are you okay?" Kendal's voice softened. "I mean, really."

"Yeah, fine. It'll just take a little getting used to. You know, being alone again, that's all."

"I know this isn't easy. But if you don't do it now, then all your hard work will be for nothing. We need this separation—even if it terrifies us. Derek, you know I'm here for you. If you need anything, just let me know, okay?"

"Yeah, okay, sure. See you tomorrow."

He disconnected and threw the cellphone on the bed. He wasn't convinced this was the best way for him to get his life on track. Not if he wanted her in it. He thought they should be working it out together. But Kendal had other ideas. She thought that he needed to figure things out for himself. Especially the way he had been acting lately.

Maybe she's right, he thought.

He looked around his massive master bedroom, then walked over to the expansive window overlooking the lights of the city below. He stood staring out in silent contemplation. He wondered what the reaction to his tattoos was going to be when he walked into his office Monday morning.

Looking up at the new moon, he caught the reflection of himself standing in the window. He no longer feared the physical transformation he was going through. Instead, he felt apprehension for what was yet to come.

He removed his shirt in front of the dressing mirror to study the elaborate ink that had taken over his body. It had been a while since he had felt the urge to revisit these markings, and he was both fascinated and frightened by their beauty. He ran his fingers over the intricate patterns, tracing the curves and swirls, feeling the imaginary warmth of the ink radiating up his arm.

He hadn't felt like this since that terrible night when the tattoos had taken over his body. The symptoms resurfaced like a wave of nausea, dread mixed with anticipation, and he knew that something was about to change. He tried to hold onto the sensation, to savor its intensity, but it was gone too soon.

Derek stepped back from the mirror. He needed to find out what the tattoos meant, why they had appeared. And he knew, to his great dismay, that the answers lay somewhere outside the confines of this room.

His thoughts drifted to his mentor, Dr. Christopher Casey, and what he might have thought about his appearance and the idea of relinquishing part of the practice to his colleagues. Derek's partners had become increasingly disenfranchised with the way the business was being operated. He imagined how they'd react when they saw him for the first time. He felt his pulse quicken and his throat tighten.

With one last glance in the mirror, he turned his focus to his department-store-style walk-in closet and felt a little of the tension start to dissipate. The perfectly pressed color-coordinated shirts and pants hung on one side, with his name-brand tailored suits and tuxedos on the other. At the end of the closet, he picked up a handmade Italian shoe. Setting the shoe back in place, he turned to grab a pair of jeans, a shirt, and tie then flipped off the light. He set the clothes on his dressing table and climbed into bed.

Derek spent a restless night, his eyes fluttering open and closed as fragmented thoughts and visions tumbled through his mind. He awoke when the first light of dawn seeped through the sheer curtains that draped the window. He stumbled out to the kitchen. The penthouse filled with silence. The stillness pressed in on him. The chill of the night still lingered in the air.

The hardwood and stone floors led to a massive kitchen, unused and abandoned. Its stainless-steel appliances gleamed in the natural light, the quartz countertops shining like diamonds. It was a stark contrast to Kendal's little kitchen—as if someone had carefully preserved the room, a museum to the man he used to be. The kitchen floor felt cool under his bare feet as he entered.

A deep-seated memory bubbled to the surface. His mother had dreamed of a kitchen like this when they had struggled to make ends meet. She had said that one day she would have a fancy kitchen, where she could cook and entertain guests. But that day never came. Instead, their fate had intervened—his father's terminal illness, his near-death beating—it all seemed so tragic. And now she was gone as well. Time lost never to be recaptured.

He opened the cupboards one by one, hoping to find some kind of sustenance, but every shelf was bare. A wave of dread washed over him as he realized that there was nothing to eat or drink in the house.

He walked over to the pantry, running his fingers along the smooth wooden shelves that held nothing but a thin layer of dust. A single wine bottle sat in the corner. He picked it up, turning it over in his hands.

A sudden wave of grief washed over him as he clutched the wine bottle to his chest. He had missed out on so much. His mother had been a victim, too. Why had he blamed her? He missed her so much, her warm smile and her laughter. Now, standing in this abandoned kitchen, Derek felt closer to her than he had in all his adult years.

He set the wine bottle back on the shelf and swung open the large stainless-steel refrigerator door to find a bright white, bare vault. It was a stark representation of the life he had returned to—the emptiness that stemmed from his previous dysfunctional world. His old life had every trapping of success—money, professional acclaim, the right car, the right clothes—yet he'd had no real friends. No one to cook for. No one to love. No one to miss him when he was gone.

Derek closed the refrigerator door in disgust and went to get dressed.

Wind rushed against his skin as he rode his motorcycle along the California coast. He rode hard, pushing the bike to its limits and taking in the panoramic views. The sun shone brightly, casting a golden hue over everything, and the smell of the ocean filled his nose. He felt free and alive.

Riding the bike was his only respite from the helter-skelter world in which he now lived—and from the countless surgeries he used to perform, his loneliness, and the chaos of his own memories. He knew he could never truly escape, not really, but it allowed him to forget for a little while.

The road ahead stretched out before him, enticing him to take a chance and see what lay beyond. He opened the throttle and let the engine roar as the bike sped forward, faster and faster until his heart was pounding in his chest. The vibrations of the engine coursed through him as he flew over the asphalt. It was exhilarating and liberating.

Derek felt alive. He felt as if he could ride forever in control of his destiny with no fear of what the future may bring.

He rode until the sun began to set, and then reluctantly made his way back home. He had found peace for now on the open road, and he knew he'd be back soon to reconnect with life.

Chapter 2

Kendal sat motionless on the couch in her living room, her finger still hovering over the button that had disconnected the call. She closed her eyes, wishing silently that she could understand what Derek was going through.

Something in his voice worried her. He sounded worn down, almost like he had given up. It was a defeatist attitude that had started gradually but had become increasingly apparent over the last few weeks.

Derek had never been the easygoing, jovial type, but he had a sense of humor. Usually, he would at least attempt to join in when someone was trying to cheer him up. Now, he was just so apathetic and disconnected. He'd reverted back to his old cynical self—possibly worse. He'd stopped connecting with her, simply going through the motions of conversation without any emotion. It seemed as if a dark cloud of self-pity had taken over his attitude.

It had only been a few hours since Derek had left. She looked around her little apartment, now sadly empty. When he had first arrived, it felt so cramped with another person staying in such a small space, but now it suddenly felt hollow without his things laying around.

Gone were the piles of books he'd amassed to research his tattoos, the scattered silly trinkets they had bought together, and the small, framed photo of them at the beach that she'd kept on the dresser—and that he had grabbed on the way out. She found herself missing the smell of his cologne, a trace of which still lingered in the air.

Kendal went to the kitchen to make a cup of tea, her mind going over all the conversations they had shared in this very room. He had been gone for such a short time, yet the apartment felt like it had lost a part of itself.

She remembered the morning he had stumbled into the clinic covered head to toe in tattoos. She hadn't recognized him at first. What a crazy thing to happen. Yet she didn't regret letting him come home with her. He had nowhere else to go. It now felt like an honor to be the one he had turned to in his hour of need. But she had done all she could do for him. It was time that he tried to take care of himself. Derek and his problems had become more than she could handle.

After their last large argument, Kendal asked him to leave. Derek had gathered his things soon after. She hadn't heard from him, so she made the call to ensure he was all right. She got up from the couch and walked over to the little kitchen window to look out at the deck where they had spent so many hours talking.

All that remained now were memories of their time together. She had always been aware of the possibility that Derek would have to leave, but not this way. He had left so upset she knew it was the best thing for him, *and for her,* yet this sense of finality was overwhelming. She wished he had told her the many things that were going on in his head. He had once again become the stranger she had let into her home.

But he had become an intimate person for a while. He had successfully been able to maintain a connection with her. They would sit on the deck of the small apartment, watching the sun slowly sink below the horizon, still and peaceful, almost as if time was standing still save for the occasional chirp of a bird or hum of a bee. They spent hours talking about anything and everything, and she had felt an almost magical sense of comfort coming from him.

But his worries and insecurities were like a contagion, stirring the fears and hurt Kendal had buried deep inside. She'd tried to shake it off, but it was like a dark shadow that followed her everywhere, a reminder of all she'd gone through before moving to California—and all that she thought she had escaped.

Now Derek was gone. All that remained in her heart were memories. Memories of a lazy Sunday spent in bed, of long conversations until the sun rose in the sky—of laughter and what she thought was love.

She walked into the bedroom and her heart sank. The sheets were rumpled and twisted, as if a body had been there only moments before. It felt like a silent accusation, a reminder of past nights. She swallowed hard, throat tight, and began to strip the sheets off.

As she worked, she could smell his scent swirl around her like a mist of regret. Despite the evidence of Derek's presence, it felt strangely as if she had grasped at a dream. She pulled the comforter off, and suddenly a wave of emotion overcame her. The smell of him filled the room, and memories of all the previous nights came flooding back. Tears tumbled down her cheeks.

On autopilot, she stripped the bed clean, planning to wash the linens and the quilted throw. Going through this mundane task was her way of saying goodbye, of wiping their intimate time together away from her memory. Of cleansing him from her inner soul.

Right after she had told Derek that he needed to leave her apartment and go back home, Kendal watched him pacing around the apartment. His eyes darted to the door every few seconds like a wary animal, and his breathing was shallow and quick. He kept running his hands over his scalp, as if trying to sort out the thoughts that were spinning in his head.

Kendal knew something was wrong, he wasn't in his right mind. It all felt so out of control, it was starting to scare her. She worried about what he might do next. Derek had retreated deeply and completely back into himself. He had always been a loner, but lately she had seen a fearfulness in him that hadn't been there before. It was clear to her that the tattoos had taken root in him, something he either couldn't or wasn't able to express. All he'd tell her was that he struggled with feelings of insignificance and inadequacy, emotions that had plagued him for years. Without the proper tools he would never be able to communicate his struggles or put them in perspective.

This is when she knew she was in over her head. He needed professional help. He needed to go back to Dr. Margaret Cole, the psychologist and life coach, who could help him make sense of his current situation.

During one of his tirades, Kendal had approached him cautiously, gently placing her hand on his arm. She knew this could make him upset, but she had to try. "Derek," she said softly. "Please, tell me what's wrong. Maybe I can help."

She studied his profile as he stared out the window, her heart aching for the way his brow furrowed, and the lines that formed around his mouth. Despite wanting to reach out and comfort him, she couldn't bring herself to do it. She wanted to make his pain go away, but in the absence of any words from him, she felt helpless.

Derek had turned his head to look at her, his eyes dark with rage. For a moment, Kendal felt a stab of fear. She drew her hand back. She thought he might grab her, or even worse. His reaction had scared her and reinforced her decision to send him packing.

In the end, Derek had shaken his head, his face a mask of determination. "You can't help me," he said, his voice barely above a whisper. "I know I have to do this by myself."

With that, he had turned and left the apartment, leaving Kendal alone, confused, shaken, and feeling guilty for not being able to help him. As she stood in her living room, frozen in fear, she thought, "He will never be able to tell me the truth about what is really going on in his mind."

That was when she had made her final decision to ask him to leave.

Kendal understood there was something more going on with him than their failed romantic relationship. Much more than just him being removed from her apartment and being sent back to his penthouse. But Derek wasn't ready to open up about it. All she could do was be patient and wait for him to be ready to talk. To be his friend. Until then, she could do nothing but worry and hope that he would eventually come out of this current turmoil that was going on in his mind. He had done it once before—she had seen him do it.

Unfortunately, this time seemed different. It was clear to her that something had taken root in him, something he either couldn't or wouldn't express. All he'd tell her was that he felt insignificant and inadequate, two emotions he had been grappling with for years without ever being able to properly communicate them or put them in perspective.

Kendal walked into the bathroom and pulled his towel from the towel rack. She picked up the sheets and comforter that she'd thrown on the floor, then grabbed her wallet off the dresser. She looked back at the bed, now stripped bare. It reflected how she felt. She proceeded down to her building's laundry room. The lights automatically flickered on. She stuffed the oversized load into the machine.

She stood listening to the hum of the washer and thought that every time they tried talking about it, something held him back and it turned into an argument. He acted as if he were afraid of being judged or revealing too much of himself to her. He had built a wall around his feelings, and it seemed to be getting thicker and harder to penetrate as time passed.

Kendal was worried; she wanted to help him the best that she could. She knew she had to be patient and understanding, yet she felt helpless when faced with his unexpressed pain.

She reminded herself that all she could do was to be there for him, listening and providing the support and validation he needed to start healing. She couldn't do it for him. That is why she had sent him back home. She was beginning to bear the burden of his recovery as if it were her responsibility, and that wasn't healthy.

She prayed that in a few months, things would improve. When she first told him that she wanted him to leave her apartment and go back to his own home, Derek seemed to admit he was struggling. After talking to him tonight, she could see he had a long way to go. Right now, she had to be content with knowing that he had started to take the necessary steps to take control back in his life.

Kendal left the laundry room with her sheets and comforter folded and smelling of fabric softener. She slowly climbed the stairs back to her apartment. Her cockatoo, Brutus, screeched on his perch when she walked back into her apartment. She covered his cage and went into her bedroom to remake the bed and put Derek's towel back in the closet.

Chapter 3

The bell clanged as the door opened to the Tremendous Tattoo Shop. A young, tall, athletic-looking Asian man stood in the entrance, his broad shoulders almost the width of the door. He wore a plain white T-shirt, black jeans, and a leather jacket. He had a small backpack slung over one shoulder.

The young man stepped inside, slowly taking in his surroundings. The shop was small and dark, with colorful flash art and graffiti artwork hung on the walls. A few old swivel chairs were scattered around. Behind a small counter was a glass display case showcasing various tattoo supplies, and several framed photographs of customers' ink.

The room was lined with tattoo stations. The young man stood silently waiting until Terry emerged from behind a bead curtain and pulled an unlit cigar stub from his mouth. "How can I help you?"

"I'm not sure." The young man's eyes darted around.

"Then why don't you start by telling me what brought you in?" Terry asked in a gravelly voice.

"Well," he took a half-step forward, "I have been out of the country for a while, and I was hoping to get a little advice."

"I'll do my best." Terry gestured with the cigar butt. "Have a seat. Tell me what's on your mind."

"I'm not quite sure where to start." His tall frame sank down on one of the swivel chairs.

"What's your name, son?"

"Tyler."

"What brought you into my shop, Tyler?" Terry prodded.

"My tattoos—" He hesitated, seeming unsure what to say next.

"And where are these tattoos?" Terry's words tumbled out like rocks from the back of his throat.

With finesse, his hands moved slowly. "On my torso, arms and legs," he said softly.

"And what kind of tattoos are they?" Terry tried to soften his abrasive manner to mirror the mild-mannered tone of the young man.

He looked around. "Magical tattoos," in a confidential tone.

"Don't worry, we're alone," Terry reassured him. "Magical tattoos, huh?"

"Yes." He bowed his head as if in prayer.

Terry straightened his back. "Well, if you already have magical tattoos, why are you coming to see me?" He jammed the cigar stub back in his mouth.

The young man looked up. "Because my magical tattoos are wanted by other people for bad things. I am not sure what to do." His eyes had a lost, boyish look.

"I still don't understand, why would you come into my shop?" Terry rubbed his hand across the back of his neck. He was starting to feel uncomfortable with the situation. He didn't like getting emotionally involved in other people's business.

"I don't know, I was passing and saw your sign and thought maybe this was where I was supposed to come for help." An anguished look passed over his face. He closed his eyes and swallowed hard. He looked like he was going to be sick.

"So, where did you get these magical tattoos?" Terry's forceful voice reverberated throughout the room, hoping to snap the young man out of his emotional state.

With a solemn expression he answered, "Thailand."

"Are you from Thailand?"

"No, I'm from California," he replied weakly.

"How did you end up getting magical tattoos in Thailand?"

He looked Terry in the eye. "My father is military, and my mother is from Thailand. I went back to stay with a cousin last year who is into Thai martial arts. I became very involved, and one thing led to another, and I decided to get the tattoos." He glanced away.

"So, why are you having problems now?" Terry held his focus on the young man sitting in front of him.

"When I came back," he sighed audibly, "I found my younger brother in some serious financial trouble. He's into some dangerous stuff and now he has involved me, and I don't know what to do."

"Why don't you just go to your family?" Terry watched Tyler's body language for any indications of deception.

"These people have already threatened me and my brother, Jason. I want to keep the rest of my family as far away from this as possible."

"So, what do these people want from you?"

"They believe that my tattoos will give them the things that they desire." He hugged himself. "I can't be a part of that."

"So, if you don't go along with what they want, they're threatening you?" Terry chewed on his cigar stub, contemplating the situation.

"Yes, they will kill my brother." Tyler's face wrenched.

"How did they find out about your magical tattoos?"

"I believe my brother told them out of self-preservation. I think

Jason may have offered me up in exchange to settle his debt." A sad look came over his face.

Shoulders squared, Terry raised his eyebrows. "So, where's your brother now?"

"I don't know." Tyler embraced himself, almost as if he was trying to protect his own body. "They kidnapped him from his apartment."

"Whoa." Terry pulled his cigar back out of his mouth. "That doesn't sound good."

"These people really mean business." Tyler's arms tightened around his body.

"Have you thought about going to the police?"

"Yes, but what am I going to tell them?" His face contorted like he wanted to cry. "That a gang kidnapped my brother because he owes them money and now they want me to fight for them because of my magical tattoos?" His hands fell back down to his lap in defeat.

"I see what you mean." Terry rubbed his chin. "I have a friend that just went through an unusual experience, he might have some suggestions. Let me give him a call."

From behind the hanging beads in the doorway, Terry observed the tall young man on the edge of the chair. He hit Derek's number and listened to it ring.

"Hello?'

"Hey, Doc, It's Terry. I have someone here that needs your help. Do you think you can come down and talk to this kid?"

Derek sounded eager to leave wherever he was. "Sure, Terry, when?"

"Well, right now if you can, it sounds like the kid is in a bit of trouble."

"Okay, give me a few minutes."

"Great. Thanks, Doc."

Terry tucked his phone into his pocket, then cast a glance back through the beaded curtain. The young man was still immobile, gaze transfixed like he'd been hypnotized.

"Do you think I could take a look at your magical tattoos?" Terry sat down on a swivel stool. "I've only seen them in books."

"Sure."

"And my name is Terry Ford, I'm the owner of this fine establishment." He rolled his stool closer to shake the young man's hand.

Tyler stood and shook Terry's hand, then slowly took off his jacket, folded it and gently laid it on the back of the chair in the tattoo station next to them. He removed his oversized shirt to reveal the intricate designs on his chiseled torso.

"This was all done by hand?" Terry stared, amazed, chewing hard on his cigar.

"Yes. At the temple." Tyler looked back over his shoulder.

"How long did it take?" Terry stepped a little closer to examine the figures, also known as sacred geometry.

"About six months. I would go to prayer ceremonies where they used special needles for the spiritual application process."

"This is magnificent." He tilted his head forward to take a closer look.

"Yes, it is quite sacred and involves a great amount of work and prayer," Tyler said, feeling a bit exposed as he turned to display the front of his torso.

"What made you want to do this?" Terry straightened and stepped back.

Tyler looked Terry squarely in the eyes. "My faith."

"Your faith in what?" Terry regarded him quizzically.

He answered in a firm voice. "God."

"Ah, I see." He nodded.

Tyler sat back down. The front door opened with a clang, and into the room walked a man of medium height, illustrated with tattoos and wearing a baseball cap. He seemed to carry with him an atmosphere of familiarity, though the precise origin of his acquaintance was not immediately clear. The light streaming in through the door revealed intricate tattoos on his face and neck that continued down beneath his white T-shirt.

"Hey, Doc. How are you doing? This is my new friend, Tyler Harris. Tyler, this is Dr. Derek Hollinger. I call him Doc."

Derek shifted his attention to Tyler's fully illustrated torso, then gave him a two-finger wave. "Hello." He let the door close behind him. Facing Terry, his eyes widened. "What do we have here?"

"Magical tattoos." Terry gave a Cheshire Cat smile. "Tyler has been to Thailand and received his tattoos at the temple. There is a very sacred ritual you must go through to receive these very special tattoos."

"Really?" Derek looked over at Tyler. "Wow, very impressive." He turned back to Terry. "What can I do for you?"

"Not quite sure yet, he has a problem with these tattoos. Thought it might be up your alley."

"What kind of problem?" Derek furrowed his brows, making the lines of the tattoos on his own face come together in a unique geometrical pattern.

Terry walked back and pointed, "You tell him, Tyler."

After hearing Tyler's story, Derek decided it was best to bring

Tyler back to the penthouse. As they pulled into the garage, he motioned for Tyler to park his crotch-rocket Kawasaki motorcycle next to his Harley. The super sport bike with its lightweight high-speed, high-performance engine was the extreme opposite of the classic cruiser style of the Harley sitting next to it.

Cocking his head toward the Harley, while attaching his helmet to his bike, Tyler asked, "This yours?"

Derek slid out from behind the wheel of his Bentley. "Yeah, I ride a little."

"Nice." Tyler said with a low whistle as he took off his leather jacket.

"I enjoy it when I can," Derek said, motioning for Tyler to follow as he proceeded toward a large set of double glass doors. He punched in a security code, the doors slid open, then closed with a thud behind them as they walked through the echo chamber of the massive marble lobby.

The uniformed guard behind the security desk raised his head and smiled a big, white-toothed smile. "Good evening, Dr. Hollinger."

Derek appreciated the greeting. The men who worked the security desk had been supportive after he explained the bizarre situation— that he had gone to sleep and woke up covered in a bodysuit of tattoos. They'd known him for years, and even though the story was pretty wild, the guards knew he hadn't been covered in ink before.

"Hey, Sam how are you doing this evening?" Derek looked over at the security desk and pushed the elevator button.

"Very well, Doc. I think I passed my exams last week, just waiting for the results."

Derek pointed at him and smiled. "I have all the faith in you. You'll be done before you know it."

"It already feels like it's been *forever*." Sam stood looking over the desk at the two men. "Just one more semester and I can graduate with my degree. Then I get ready for the bar."

The elevator door opened. Derek motioned for Tyler to step in.

"That's going to be the easy part for you," Derek said.

"Yeah, well, from your mouth to God's ears." Sam laughed.

"Catch you later," Derek said as the elevator doors closed.

"How long have you lived here?" Tyler asked, watching the floor numbers flash past on the panel.

"Almost ten years. I've spent most of my time working." They stepped out of the elevator. "But recently I decided to make it a little homier." He stuck his key in the door and pushed it open, then stepped aside and waited for Tyler to enter. The young man looked up at the massive, vaulted ceilings, then walked over to one of the expansive windows to admire the view.

"Can I get you something to drink?" Derek asked, walking into the kitchen.

"No, thanks, not right now." Tyler turned from the window to scan the refined but stylish furnishings.

"Over here is the balcony." Derek opened the oversized glass door. "I just put this furniture out here and they delivered the palms this afternoon. I think it turned out pretty well." He stepped out onto the balcony. "What do you think?"

"Yeah, nice." Tyler followed.

Derek pulled out one of the patio chairs from under the table. He brushed off the cushion and sat down. "Sit, sit."

Tyler pulled out a chair, sat down, and stared at the ground.

Breaking the silence, Derek began, "Okay, I know you're worried about your brother. Why don't you start back at the beginning?"

Derek watched Tyler's smooth, hairless face while he ran his fingers through his short, jet-black hair. He could see the weight of the problem on Tyler's shoulders and sensed that he was struggling with the decision to enlist help.

"Listen, Tyler, I know this must be very difficult for you. I can't imagine what an awesome responsibility you are feeling right now for your brother's safety. But you're going to have to trust someone. I believe I can be objective. I have had a lot of trials and tribulations lately myself. Run it back by me; if I can help, I will."

Tyler leaned forward in his chair, clasping his hands together. "I just got back from Thailand last night. My brother was supposed to pick me up. When he didn't show up at the airport, well, I knew something was wrong. So I just went straight to his apartment."

He sat back in the chair, hands balled into fists under his arms. "When I got there, I walked in on a couple of guys trashing the place. They told me that he owed them money, and that if he didn't pay them something bad was going to happen to him. Then they knocked me out." He grabbed the hair on the top of his head with both hands. "Next thing I know I'm waking up with a headache and my brother asking me what happened!"

He looked over at Derek. "I asked my brother how he could owe them that kind of money. He said he had been gambling and got behind. He didn't think it was as serious as I was making it out to be." He shook his head. "I believed him. But when I got up this morning, I made a run to the corner for some coffee. Just when I was returning, I saw them putting my brother into a car and driving off."

"You saw them take your brother?" Derek cocked his head, revealing the black and red spider on his neck. It appeared to have a vicelike grip on his head.

"I saw the same guys that I had fought with struggling with someone in the backseat of a car in front of my brother's apartment. I ran to try to catch them, but they drove off. I was too late." Tyler furrowed his eyebrows to blink back tears, then swallowed hard. "Then I received a phone call. It was a ransom-type call."

Derek leaned back in his chair, looking directly into Tyler's dark brown eyes. "So how much money are they asking for?"

He held his gaze. "I wish it were that simple."

"Why?" Derek's jaw clenched. "What are they asking for?"

Tyler stuck his chin out and took a deep breath. "They want me to fight Friday night."

"Why would they want you to fight?"

"I'm not sure, but I know it has to do with my tattoos. I think they believe they will have a large element bet on me because of my magical tattoos. I don't know right now if they are betting on me to win or lose, but I do know they will have a large amount of money on me."

"Tell me about these magical tattoos," Derek said. "What makes them so magical?"

Tyler fell back in his chair, a faraway look in his eyes. "People here think this is an evil art. That it is connected to witchcraft or something. I have a deep connection to the power they imbue, but they are symbols of my spirituality and beliefs. They are a symbol of my devotion."

Derek shifted in his seat as he began to comprehend the situation. "Ah, now I understand. It's all about the gambling for them. They hit the jackpot when they discovered you."

"I guess that's a good way to put it. My brother owes them, and I offered to pay it back, but they won't accept the money." His expression was pained. "All they want is for me to fight."

"Well, yeah. If they can parlay this into something big, you can be the gift that keeps on giving," Derek said dryly.

"This goes against everything I believe, using the magical tattoos for malicious intent. That's why I went into the tattoo parlor today. I thought the quickest and easiest way would be to cover them. I will do anything to protect my brother. Then they would just have to accept the money."

"Do you think that strategy will work?"

"I'll never know. I didn't get the money. I went to my father, and he turned me down. I'm disappointed but not surprised."

"Then why are you still trying to cover the tattoos?" Derek frowned.

"I figure if the tattoos are gone, then I can negotiate some new terms with them."

Derek shook his head. "I'm not sure that's the best way to approach this. These guys seem like a pretty violent group."

Tyler stiffened against the back of the chair. "Yeah, they had guns when I ran into them in my brother's apartment. That's how they got the jump on me."

Derek held up his cellphone. "Then I think we had better call the police."

"I already thought about that." He pressed both hands on the table. "If I go to the police, what am I going to say? My brother has been gambling and owes some thugs money and now he has disappeared, and they want me to fight Friday night because I have magical tattoos?" He pursed his lips and shook his head.

"Okay, it doesn't sound too credible," Derek had to admit.

"Plus, I had asked my brother to go to the authorities when I first saw him. He said he couldn't because there is a warrant out for his arrest."

"For what?"

"He told me he has driving violations. My brother is not the most—he has a crazy history. I was hoping things had gotten better. I never should have left him behind." Tyler crossed his arms. "I should have stayed and looked after him or taken him with me."

Derek sat back, relaxing in his new chair. "How long were you in Thailand?"

Tyler looked up for a second, calculating. "Almost two years."

"What made you go over there in the first place?"

Tyler sighed heavily, staring out at the distant horizon as he recalled the last time he had seen his mother. He had been a very young man with a wild heart, full of dreams and big ideas but a limited bank account. His mother was struggling financially, and he felt bad because he couldn't help.

Even worse, his mother and brother had fought all the time. When Tyler saw an opportunity to go to Thailand and chase adventure, he had taken it, leaving them behind without looking back.

Now here he was back home, the scene of so much strife and grief. He had thought he was running away from it all, but now he realized he was just running away from himself. He wanted to make things right, to try and make amends for his mistakes. He wanted to finally find peace. He was determined to come home, and this time, *really come home*. He had to find a way to help his brother.

"More reasons than I can explain right now," he finally answered.

"When you went there, did you plan to stay for two years?" Derek persisted.

"No way." He shook his head. "I had planned a two-week vacation." He slumped his arms onto the table and interlaced his fingers. "Then I ran into my cousin who's around my age, and he brought me into the Muay Thai world. We began training at the gym with his instructor who took me under his wing. Muay Thai consumed my life while I was there; it completely changed me. Before I traveled to Thailand, I didn't have any spiritual understanding. Now I have a strong spiritual awareness that guides all of my decisions."

"I get what you're saying." Derek thought about his own recent discovery of spiritual awareness.

"I've gone through my own transformation," Tyler continued, "and now I need to figure out how to save my brother."

"Where are you staying?"

"I haven't figured that out yet. I can't go back to my brother's place. I don't want to go to my mom's, and, well . . . my father is out of the question."

"You can stay here," Derek offered as he got up from the table.

"No, I can't impose on you." Tyler jumped up from his chair to follow.

"Sure, you can." He entered the penthouse through the huge glass balcony door. "You see the size of this place. It's just me here." He pointed to the kitchen. "I just bought groceries."

Tyler made a slight bow at the waist. "Thank you for your generosity."

"We need to do some strategic planning." Derek led him back into the penthouse and down a long hall. "You can go ahead and get comfortable. I have some things I need to take care of. Let's go back over everything tonight and figure out the best way to move forward."

As they passed, Tyler stopped to look into one of the open bedroom doors. "Yeah okay. Thank you, Dr. Hollinger," he said, rushing to catch back up.

"Listen, you can call me Derek or Doc. That's it," he called back over his shoulder.

"Okay, thanks, Doc."

"That's better. And if those guys call you again, don't commit to anything until we figure out the next move." Derek stopped and turned. "Does that sound okay with you?"

"Yeah, sure."

"Right in here." Derek pointed into a guest suite.

Tyler stepped into the luxurious suite, his feet sinking into the plush carpet. He couldn't help but feel a pang of nostalgia for his childhood bedroom. Taking a couple of seconds to inspect his surroundings, he turned back toward the door and found he was alone.

Derek had already left.

Chapter 4

"Hello, Derek, it's nice to see you. It's been a while." Dr. Cole leaned back in her chair and brushed back a lock of short-cropped gray hair with one slender finger. "How have you been dealing with your return to work?" Her light green eyes studied his face.

"It's been a real challenge." Derek sat gripping the chair's arms like it was about to take off. "People don't treat me the way they used to. Everything is different. People I've known for years suddenly look at me like I'm a stranger. People in the office avoid talking to me. I had a gentleman refuse to shake my hand the other day." His tattooed head dropped, shaking back and forth. "It's humiliating."

He hesitated, then leaned forward. "I have collaborated in consultations with the two doctors who work with me in my business and their patients have made it obvious they are very uncomfortable just having me in the room. They avoid any type of eye contact and direct their questions to the other two doctors.

"When I come into work, I still have Kendal." His back stiffened. "She's supportive, but she doesn't want to have that close relationship anymore. She believes I need to take care of some emotional issues first. And now that I'm back to work, I can see she is probably right.

"Some days I feel so lost . . ." He rubbed the back of his neck. "I truly don't know. I feel sick all the time. I worry constantly that I am going to destroy my practice. I try to tell myself everything is going to be all right, but then I experience a negative reaction from someone that sends me right back into a tailspin."

His hand came down to rub his chest. "I'm starting to have anxiety attacks again. I can't sleep."

"First," Dr. Cole leaned forward with her hands cupped together on her desk, "this internal conflict that you are experiencing is normal. But you can't worry about what people are thinking or you *will* make yourself sick."

"That's not the worst part. I have had a lot of the tattoos come back." He pulled down his shirt collar to show a new pattern of spiral ink.

"In extreme cases like yours, one can continue to manifest symptoms."

"I don't understand." He ground his teeth in frustration. "I was doing so well, and they were starting to disappear! Now I feel like I am right back where I started."

"Sometimes we must take a step back and evaluate before moving forward again. I understand the changes of your body can be alarming. You are equating your physical appearance with your identity. This is where you decide what you must learn about yourself. You should be experiencing a period of enlightenment and realization. It all goes back to connecting your thoughts to your actions. You are literally what you think about. In your case it manifests itself like a tapestry on your skin.

"Think about this—material gain can come from different sources, money, title, trophies, etc. Your stature is a collective recognition. You've earned yours through years of arduous labor. But in that recognition may emerge the danger of an *elevated stature* that people created for you. They imagine what you should be and project a grandiose image, seeing you as greater than them. When that image comes crashing down, you are now forced to face your identity. If that identity isn't compatible with what the world perceives, then that is where your struggle lies."

Derek leaned forward in his chair. He could sense she was on to something.

"You are still in the process of trying to figure out who you are and what your identity should be. You have been caught up in the glory of stature and now it's time to get in touch with the inner you, the soul, your foundation. Being a doctor is your profession. It's not who you are, *it's what you do*."

"That's the hardest part." Derek shook his head. "I thought I liked who I was. I worked hard to become a doctor. I had a calm, quiet life. This change feels more like a bad dream. It happened so quickly. Now I'm feeling boxed in. I still have the obligations, but I don't belong anymore. The place where I live, I don't feel welcome there.

"I have people who count on me for a living but don't respect me. When I was living with Kendal, it felt like I had a home with a future. A future with free will where I could make anything happen. Now that I have come back to my everyday life, I feel trapped. The expectations make me question what that purpose should be now."

Dr. Cole nodded. "That's understandable."

"One of the things I've realized is that I don't need all the material things. I don't want to go back to my old life. Living with Kendal helped me to see that there is much more to life than just material trappings. I know we were brought together under unusual circumstances, but that doesn't mean it should ruin our fate or destiny, does it?"

Dr. Cole smiled. "If you feel that your destiny is to be with this woman, then you should concentrate on doing everything in your power to prepare yourself to make that happen. Then again, you may come to the realization that she's not your destiny."

"I've been trying to figure out how all of this is linked," Derek said.

"Linked?"

"Well, there are strong connections happening. Like fate. When Kendal and I went down to San Diego to work for the homeless, I ran into Spider, the guy who tried to beat me to death."

As a teenager, Derek had been attacked and suffered severe injuries at the hands of a gang. The silver lining is that it was how he met his mentor, Dr. Christopher Casey, who performed multiple reconstructive surgeries on him. Over the early years of Derek's recovery, they'd grown very close and Dr. Casey took him under his wing. It was why Derek became a plastic surgeon.

"Really?" Dr. Cole said with interest. "How did that come about?"

"I was working in the medical tent across from where he was attending a revival. I happened to go over there to check out the sermon when I recognized him."

"What did you do when you realized it was the man who tried to kill you?"

"At first, I was shocked. It took a minute for it to sink in. I actually had to walk out of the tent. Truthfully, it had never crossed my mind that I would ever run into him. Then I realized this might be the only chance I would get to confront him. I decided to go back. I just walked up to him and asked him if he recognized me."

"What did he say?"

Derek shook his head. "He didn't even recognize me or blink an eye when I told him who I was and what he had done to me."

"How did that make you feel?"

"Angry at first." He drummed his fingers on the edge of the chair's arm. "But then I continued to talk to him and realized that his life had pretty much amounted to zero and he was nothing but a pathetic old man. Father Mike, who was the preacher giving the sermon, told me that Spider had just been released from prison with a diagnosis of liver cancer. Once that information started to sink in, it occurred to me that this man was already marked for death.

"I had given him much more power than he deserved. He had taken my childhood away from me, but now I had the ability to decide whether he was going to continue to affect my future or not. He had destroyed his own life as well, a lifetime spent in prison." Derek sat up straighter. "After seeing what a pathetic, broken-down old man he was, I decided right there that he was not going to get any more of my time or energy."

"That sounds very positive."

"It was. That was the first time I slept through the night without any nightmares. I also lost a couple more of my tattoos."

"So, you say you lost a couple *more* tattoos. You had seen a change previous to this?"

"Yes. I had one that disappeared from around my ankle when Kendal and I first got together. Then the next time was when I saw Spider."

"Do you think there is a connection to these two events?"

He rubbed his chin. "Not between the events themselves. But I do see that when I tap in, or face a feeling and explore that feeling, it seems to release something in me."

"And that release seems to erase or diminish the tattoos?"

"Maybe." He shrugged. "I haven't quite figured it out."

Dr. Cole studied him. "Overall, how are you feeling with your emotional progress?"

"It's a roller coaster ride," he replied ruefully. "Some days I'm ready to give up, and then something positive happens. There are days when I feel like I can do nothing to improve things. But then I think that if I don't continue to fight and figure out what is making these things manifest on me, I will never be able to move forward."

"Have you spent any more time thinking about your beliefs and where you stand on faith or your spirituality?"

Derek nodded. "I have a meeting coming up with Father Mike. He was kind enough to offer to stop by and see me, and I will have another conversation with him."

"Good," she said firmly. "I believe you will find that the more you establish a spiritual belief system, the more solid your foundation will become. Make sure you make another appointment on your way out."

Arriving back at the penthouse, Derek found the place quiet. As he passed through the kitchen, he glanced out the window and saw Tyler sitting cross-legged on the ground in meditation. Derek quietly stepped out to the balcony and sat down to enjoy the solace of the moment. He could feel the calm, soothing energy. He wondered if this might be a practice he should consider.

Tyler took a deep breath, exhaled very slowly, then stood up and stretched.

"You look refreshed," Derek said.

"Yes, meditation puts me in a better state of mind."

"I was starting to get to that point when I was living at Kendal's, but since I came back here, I seem to have lost it."

Tyler took a deep breath. "Just clear your mind and concentrate on your breath, then it all starts to happen."

Derek smiled. "I just need to stop and take the time to actually do it. Seeing you out here makes me realize this is the perfect place."

Tyler looked up to the sky, then closed his eyes. "I like to be outside." He inhaled deeply again. "I'm more relaxed when I can be closer to nature."

"So, what solutions have you come up with?"

"I've put it in the system and am waiting for results." Tyler smiled back.

"Tell me a little bit about your experience in Thailand. How did the tattooing start?"

Tyler sat down in one of the chairs. "My cousin and I would hang out at a little platform stage where some of the Muay Thai fighters from the area would train. At first, I just went there to watch. But then I started sparring and eventually worked up to competitive fighting. The local monks in the area would come to watch. They didn't mingle or speak to anyone. They would just observe. I was told they were there to pray for the fighters.

"After a while, I was approached by one of the monks. He told me that I was one of the chosen few to receive their blessing with the tattoos. At first, I wasn't sure I wanted to be a part of it. But after they explained the meaning and the importance of the offer, I decided to go along with it."

"What did they tell you?"

"They said that the person who had these tattoos would have to strictly adhere to their observances. I couldn't talk to anyone for three days after each ceremony. They said I'd been chosen because I did not display any pride or arrogance when I competed, and that when they prayed, I was shown to be obedient. For the power to be established, there are certain personality traits that must go along with the magical tattoos to keep them in force and powerful. It is looked upon as very sacred and there was a lot of physical and spiritual training that went along with the honor of accepting the tattoos." Tyler sighed. "To be honest, it was a long excruciating process."

He stretched his legs out, gazing at the twinkling reflection of sunlight off the windows of buildings far below. "When I first arrived there, I was restless. I was tense all the time. I had a hard time falling asleep, and when I did, I had a hard time staying asleep. I was miserable and couldn't control my emotions. I realized very quickly that I had anger issues, and it was destroying my peace and happiness. It was blocking me from spiritual progress and from setting any spiritual goals. If I expected to improve my mind or achieve any enlightenment, I had to submit completely."

"I can relate to that," Derek admitted.

"I realized that the most harmful effect of my anger was the illusion of being a victim and looking for revenge, always thinking that people had harmed me in some way and wanting to retaliate.

"I ultimately came to the conclusion that I had lost my freedom of choice and had been abandoned by everyone, especially my family. At least, I thought I had been abandoned. But once I let go of the anger and achieved full enlightenment, I received joy and love back into my life. Coming back here to the remnants of my old life and, unfortunately, my brother's situation reflects the turmoil I left behind. But I'm sure that is why I felt compelled to return."

"I hope it's that simple." Derek smiled.

"It will be. I must find the right answer. It will come."

"I am happy to hear that you have that kind of confidence. That is what I need to learn—to stay positive in the face of adversity."

"I can only find it while remaining balanced with my physical and spiritual being," Tyler said.

"So are you a Buddhist?"

"No," he said thoughtfully. "I sat side by side with the Buddhist monks and respected their culture and beliefs. I thought I was a Buddhist. But Jesus still lives in my heart."

"Wow, I wish I could say I had that confidence about my faith."

"You can. You just have to ask Him."

"Ask who?"

"Jesus, and the Holy Spirit."

"Ask Him what?"

"Whatever you need to know," Tyler said serenely. "He lives inside all of us."

"Interesting."

"Yeah, well, I better be moving." He stood up. "I need to get a game plan together before Friday."

"I think you should be working out." Derek looked up at him. "I might know of a place that you can use to stay in shape and stay ready to fight, just in case."

"I'm not going to fight." Tyler started to walk away.

Derek stood to follow him. "I understand, but don't you think you should be ready for all options? I'm not saying you are going to fight, but what if we need to fight our way out just to survive?"

Tyler turned quickly to look back at Derek. "What do you mean, *we?*"

"I am going to help you." Derek looked him square in the eyes.

"Oh, no, I can't allow you to get physically involved in this." Tyler shook his head.

"Don't worry. I can take care of myself. I've done a little kick-boxing." Derek released a high kick.

"Okay, spar with me," Tyler relented.

"That would be great." Derek grinned. "Let me see if I can get the place and set it up. Maybe we can go work out tomorrow night." Derek disappeared into the penthouse.

"Great, thanks," Tyler called after him.

He thought of his brother, stomach tensing with worry. *I just hope they try to contact me again.*

Chapter 5

Derek opened his front door. "Hello, Padre." He reached out to shake Father Mike's hand. "I didn't expect you so early."

"I didn't plan to be here so soon." The priest, only a few years older than him, had piercing blue eyes and dark brown hair. His jaw was stubbled, as if he hadn't shaved for a day or so. He entered the penthouse confidently as if he belonged there. "Sometimes it can take me up to four hours with traffic, but today only two and a half. I was blessed with clear sailing." He smiled.

"Welcome." Derek motioned. "Let's get comfortable. Would you like something to drink?"

"Yes, that would be wonderful, I'm parched." He wiped his brow.

"Lemonade, iced tea, a beer?" Derek called out as he walked to the kitchen.

"Iced tea would be great," Father Mike answered.

It felt good to be able to offer something to drink to a visitor in his home. Derek never realized how the small things could be so important.

"So, what's going on? I was surprised to get your call." Derek handed the glass to Father Mike, who stood admiring the panoramic view of Los Angeles.

The priest turned back to the living room. "Well, since you and I first met, a few things have transpired that I thought you should be made aware of." He slowly sat down on the edge of the fine leather high-backed chair. "Spider has collapsed into a coma and isn't expected to live. The Holy Spirit moved me to reach out to you with this information."

"That doesn't surprise me. He looked pretty bad when I saw him." Derek sat in the chair directly across from Father Mike.

"How have you been doing?" Concern swept across Father Mike's face.

"Not so good. These tattoos started to disappear and now they're back again. I'm not handling it well. My patients haven't been too receptive. My employees don't seem to trust me anymore, and my girlfriend sent me packing."

Father Mike tutted in sympathy. "Well, I am here to remind you that 'Faith is being sure of what we hope for and certain of what we do not see.' Right now, you are on a journey."

Derek gave an exasperated sigh. "And it's a very dark and scary road."

"God said, 'I will never leave you nor forsake you.' When you have God in your heart, wherever you go, He will go with you. I will pray for you. Try not to fall victim to your fears."

"It's hard not to." Derek bit his lip. "I don't know if this is ever going to end. Every day, something new happens. It's a curse."

Father Mike leaned forward in his seat. "Be very careful," he furrowed his brow, "when you buy into fear and profess 'it's a curse.' Those negative thoughts and words will control you."

His face relaxed. "But when you maintain your faith in God, you'll find a new perspective that will work to your advantage. Fear and wrong thinking are not just bad habits but are the work of the devil. Instead, when you are tempted to be discouraged, use it as a reminder to thank God and give over the control to Him."

He steepled his fingertips. "When we met at the San Diego homeless assistance event, I prayed that we would be able to get back together again. I know that was a very emotional time for you running into Spider after the horrible crime he had perpetrated on you as a child."

"I really don't care . . . but morbid curiosity makes me ask." Derek swallowed. "Where is Spider?"

"He's in the hospital under hospice care. The second reason I came to see you," he scooted to the edge of his seat, "is to ask for your help. We could really use your expertise. We are always looking for doctors who are willing to lend a helping hand. We're constantly in contact with people in need. We don't have a plastic surgeon and some of these people have birth defects or have been in an accident. Some are veterans who have fought for our country and need medical attention just to enable them to get through the simplest of tasks."

Derek nodded, thinking that maybe helping others was just what he needed. "How often would you want me to come down to San Diego?"

"As often as your time will allow. We have a small clinic, it's very basic but you are welcome to use it."

"Would you like to bring the patients up here to my clinic?"

"That would be perfect." Father Mike beamed. "God Bless you."

"Okay. Well, let's take it on a case-by-case basis. If I feel that I can handle it in your clinic, I will, and if the condition calls for a more technical environment, then we can bring them up to my clinic."

"Bless you. I know you have so much going on in your life right now."

"Yes, but maybe this will help me take my mind off my own problems for a change."

"So many people need help. A couple of weeks ago, we found an old Native woman unconscious on the floor in her motel room. It appears she was performing some type of ritual when she fell and hit her head. I have to go check on her tonight to see how she's doing." Father Mike looked sad. "I'm not sure she's going to make it; she's very weak and unresponsive. I am trying to find out if she has any family in the area. It's not likely that she comes from this area because of all the markings, you know—tattoos all over her face and arms."

"She has tattoos on her face and arms?" Derek leaned forward, suddenly alert.

"Yes. The problem is she doesn't speak English. She speaks some version of Spanish, but not a dialect that is familiar to any of our social workers. We only get bits and pieces of what she is mumbling. She goes in and out of consciousness. She has had the flu so her immune system is very weak. I believe she comes from a remote area that had not previously been exposed to our diseases. The doctors are amazed she has survived this long. Something is willing her to live. If we could only figure out what it is, maybe we could help."

Derek felt like he'd been hit by a bolt of lightning. His skin tingled and his heart raced. "Father Mike, this might be the woman that I ran into the night all of this happened to me!"

"You mean the illustrations?"

"Yes. I've said all along that I think that an old Shaman woman put a curse on me."

"Well, this woman definitely appears to be a shaman."

Derek rose and started to pace, too wound up to sit still. "How old is she?"

"Probably sixties or seventies. It's hard to say because of the culture. They live a much harder life than we do."

"This is mind-blowing. I'm telling you, this could be her! Can I come to the hospital and see her?"

Father Mike shook his head in wonder. "Who would have thought? Sure, I can meet you over at the hospital this evening. I'll try to finish my business in Los Angeles as quickly as possible, and I'll give you a call when I'm heading back down to San Diego." He made the sign of the cross. "This is a perfect example of why it's so important for us as God's servants to listen to the Holy Spirit when God speaks to us. You never know what He is trying to achieve—possibly an unexpected miracle."

Derek sat down again, his knee bouncing. "Well, if this is the old woman that did this to me, it will definitely be some kind of miracle that she is with you."

"Amen. When we maintain a union with the Holy Spirit, He serves as our conduit to God. Miracles are an everyday occurrence. Recognizing that we are more than a physical body and that we are spiritual beings filled with His light, miracles happen."

"You know. I'm not sure I understand how that works. My new friend just mentioned how Jesus lives in each one of us. How can that be?"

"The old Covenant was written on stone, you know, the Ten Commandments, which was the word of God. But the new Covenant is written on our hearts. Now, all you must do is accept Jesus, and acknowledge that He died for your sins and loves you. Read the Word, then repent of your wrong thinking and ask for forgiveness. It's just a matter of being aware. Jesus resides in everyone."

"How do I acknowledge Him?"

"First of all, repent of your sins. Then understand that the devil is a liar. He comes to lie, steal and destroy. And trust in the Lord with all your heart. Don't put your confidence in your own understanding. Let Him direct your path. By knowing that God loves you and you love thy neighbor as thyself, this becomes your testimony. You will no longer be bound by fear but by the love of God."

Derek was consumed by his thoughts, hoping that the shaman woman could undo this mess he was in. He was convinced she had the power to do so.

"It's not about your problem with the tattoos." Father Mike stared intensely into Derek's eyes, hoping to make a connection. "It's about the devil. He's a liar. He wants you to believe that you need *her* to reverse what has happened to you." He stabbed his finger into his chest with each word. "*Place your faith in Christ*. Or you can listen to the devil and continue to be deceived."

Derek met his gaze. Father Mike was starting to make him rethink his position.

"Divine versus Evil?"

"Jesus already gave his life for you. Every thought that arises from your knowledge will reveal that the strongholds are just beliefs. You don't have to hold on to something that has already been crushed. Surrender the idea that this shaman woman has some type of hold on your soul. Accept God's mercy and love."

"But I'm not worthy." Derek hung his head. "I've done nothing to deserve his love."

Father Mike placed his hand on Derek's shoulder. "Try to tell *Him* you are not worthy, when He has already given His son's life for your salvation. Don't be distracted. Tell Jesus you repent of your sins and accept Him into your heart."

Derek squeezed his eyes closed. "I do, I repent of my sins, and I accept Jesus into my heart."

"Now, tap into the truth and rejoice in your freedom. You are now brand new in the Kingdom of God. For it is written: *But whenever a person turns to the Lord, the veil is removed. Now the Lord is the Spirit and where the Spirit of the Lord is, there is freedom.*"

"How will I know?" Derek slumped back into his chair, looking up at Father Mike standing over him.

"You'll know. Don't worry. Your life won't be the same, trust me. The wisdom of God is amazing. Watch Him go to work. He is going to turn your world upside down. Communion with the Holy Spirit will lead you to a relationship with Christ. Fix your eyes not on what is seen, but on what is unseen, since what is seen is temporary, but what is unseen is eternal."

"Is this going to solve my problem with the tattoos?"

"Remember, you became self-concerned and gave the devil all the power. He finds people who will believe him, so he can steal and destroy their lives. You have a fear hiding deep within you. Now, when you fall into a flashback or a bleak memory, it will be destroyed by the Truth. When you believe Jesus is Lord and you have the Holy Spirit inside, you can stand against the tricks of the devil. You will overcome it, by your faith."

"What if it doesn't work? How do I know what the truth is?" He sighed. "I've been looking for the truth for a long time and seem to be going in circles."

"If you live by the feeling of doubt and fear, you throw your faith away. Remember, the devil wants a piece of you but when Jesus dwells in you, nothing can touch you. Possession is a stronghold that captivates your belief system, and right now you are feeling suppressed. The fear has integrated and become a part of you—the devil wants you to believe that he has all the power and the authority over what happens to you. The only thing you are experiencing is a lie, and that lie is starting to lose its power. The Truth will cut its cord and the devil will no longer have authority over you. You must hear what I am saying to you. Jesus died on the cross and has already crushed the power of the evil one."

"I'm listening," he reassured Father Mike.

"You need a strong conviction with a strong purpose. You must be a steward of your own heart. Your body is the temple and God lives in you. No matter your body's scars, the battle is already won. Jesus was physically beaten beyond recognition so that we could take on his spirit. He loved us on his worst day, the blessing is to surrender."

"I'm still not sure I know how to surrender," Derek admitted.

It felt like he'd fought for everything he wanted his whole life. Surrender was a foreign concept.

"Your greatest ally is the word. Read your Bible. Do you have a Bible?"

Derek glanced around. "Yes, somewhere."

"Eliminate self-centeredness. Create healthy and happy relationships. Read scripture, it will literally bring your soul back home." Father Mike took a step back. "I need to get going, I still have a meeting to get to. We need to continue this later."

After saying a quick prayer, the two men shook hands at the door.

Derek sat back down, feeling better than he had in a while. Yet he still couldn't help but think about the old shaman woman as he reached for his laptop. He did a Google search and scrolled through the results.

"Shamans believe that when you suffer physical or emotional trauma, a piece of your soul, or the essence, will flee your body in order to survive the experience. This life force is what keeps the body vital, alive, and thriving. A trauma could be construed as mental or physical abuse, or could be from experiencing an accident or being involved in war; being a victim of a crime or terrorist act, being caught in a natural disaster, divorce, or death of a loved one. What can cause soul loss in one individual may not cause soul loss in another. Any event that may cause shock could cause soul loss."

Derek sat staring at the screen, deep in thought, then began to read again. "A Shaman can see with the third eye or with their heart to be able to travel into the hidden realms. A Shaman believes there is a web that connects all life and the spirits that live in all things. The Shamanic journey is a major ceremony that involves an altered state of consciousness traveling outside time into the hidden realms of a parallel universe. The hidden worlds in which the Shaman resides are known as the underworld, lower-world, middle-world, and upper-world. There are numerous levels of both the lower and upper worlds that are outside of time . . ."

Derek jumped, startled by Tyler's sudden appearance.

"Sorry to bother you, I thought I would check to see if we were still on to go over to the work-out place," his new guest said with a smile.

"Oh, yeah, I have the keys."

"I'm ready if you are."

Derek jumped up from his chair. "Give me a minute to change."

Derek opened the iron gate. He and Tyler rode their motorcycles into the empty warehouse parking lot. Derek unlocked a smaller door located next to a large roll-up door and stepped inside.

It took a minute to find the light switch. This was the first time Derek had actually entered the gym. Before he woke up covered in tattoos, he had a consistent workout routine. He missed his kick-boxing classes.

He had been invited by a former patient, a professional UFC fighter, to come work out a couple of times but he had never taken him up on the offer until now. To his surprise, he found himself standing in a fully-equipped gym complete with pads on the floor, large workout ropes stretching to the ceiling, and boxing equipment hanging from the wall. He walked back out and motioned for Tyler.

"Wow, you weren't kidding when you said you had someone who could hook you up." Tyler stepped into the sprawling room, eyes wide. The mingled smell of sweat, leather and disinfectant filled his nostrils.

Derek snapped his fingers. "Okay, where do we start?"

"I like to jump rope, then do some stretches. I shadow box for about ten minutes, then I need to get a good workout on the bag. I see they have a tire over there and a few weights. I really need to get some strength training."

Once Derek realized that it wasn't necessary for him to be there, he gave Tyler the keys. He wasn't into the workout anyway, he had bigger things on his mind. He went back home to prepare to go down to San Diego.

Chapter 6

Derek felt his chest and shoulders tighten as he nervously waited for Father Mike in the lobby of the hospital. When the priest walked in wearing his black clergy shirt and pants, clasping Derek's hand and giving him a quick hug, a wave of relief washed over him. He trailed after Father Mike as they walked down the hall of the aged medical facility.

The sing-song voices of the nurses rang out, "Good evening, Father."

The weight of the situation pressed down on Derek like an invisible hand. It felt good to be with someone who was so well known. It was also evident that Father Mike was well-loved here, and Derek found himself admiring the way the priest carried himself with such ease and confidence. It was apparent that Father Mike spent a lot of time in this hospital administering to others. It solidified the feeling Derek had that Father Mike was the real deal. A man of faith who truly cared about the people he ministered to.

Father Mike stopped to put on a surgical mask and handed one to Derek. They proceeded to a closed door with contamination warnings. Father Mike opened it slowly and they stepped into the room. The sun was setting over the hospital, and the last shards of orange light beamed through the partly closed blinds of the old woman's room.

Derek strained to look past Father Mike as he pulled the curtain back from around the bed. A small form lay underneath the thin white blanket. He could see the edges of a tiny clump of black and gray hair buried inside the pillow. Father Mike stretched out a hand to rest it on the crown of her head; with the other, he motioned for Derek to come closer.

As Derek slowly rounded the end of the bed, he could see a small, wrinkled face lying on the pillow. Father Mike grabbed the chair from behind him and pulled it up. He motioned for Derek to do the same so that they both could be at face level with the bed.

Father Mike took a small bottle out of his pocket and began sprinkling the liquid around the bed, then put it back in his pocket. Pulling out a Bible, in a hushed tone he read scripture for a few minutes. Then he set the Bible on the nightstand and took another bottle, which appeared to be oil, out of his pocket. When his thumb touched her forehead, she sat straight up in bed, screeching and chanting.

Derek reared back, his heart hammering. Father Mike rebuked the devil in Jesus's name and commanded the demon to come out of her body. The old woman collapsed back into her bed. He put more oil on his thumb and made the sign of the cross on her forehead. His words were enough to bring a moment of peace to the room. This time she lay silent in her bed.

Derek sat gripping the sides of his chair, trying to understand what he had just witnessed.

Father Mike continued to read scripture. "*When an unclean spirit goes out of a man, he goes through dry places, seeking rest, and finds none. Then he says, 'I will return to my house from which I came.' And when he comes, he finds it empty, swept, and put in order. Then he goes and takes with him seven other spirits more wicked than himself, and they enter and dwell there; and the last state of that man is worse than the first. So shall it also be with this wicked generation."*

He laid the Bible in his lap and sat back in the chair. "Is this the woman you have been looking for?"

Derek studied her face, flashing back to the night when he encountered her outside the hotel . . .

An old woman approached him. Her mouth was moving, but he couldn't understand what she was saying. He looked down into her weirdly painted face just as pain exploded in his head. It felt like an ice pick being driven into his brain. Her claw-like hand grabbed his tuxedoed arm.

In a panic, Derek yanked away. The force sent the old woman sprawling to the ground. As he bent down to see if she was hurt, she reached into her bag and pulled out a rattle. She started shaking it in his face and chanting.

It sounded just like the chanting he had just heard.

"Yes." His mouth was dry. "I believe she is."

"As you can see, she is in a much-weakened state." Father Mike gazed at her with pity. "The demons keep coming, trying to take her. I must battle with them each time I come, trying to lead her to salvation. I am hoping she will have a moment of clarity so that she can accept Jesus before she passes."

"Can I talk to her?"

"You can try." Father Mike stepped out to find a nurse. Derek slid closer to the old woman.

The hallway was filled with the murmur of activity, nurses bustling around from one room to another, and the low beeping of monitors in the distance. Despite all this, Derek found himself in a moment of stillness and solitude, a respite from the chaos that had become his reality lately.

"Señora, señora," Derek whispered.

Slowly, she opened her eyes. Her black pupils were fogged white. He could see she was trying to focus. There appeared to be a hint of recognition on her face as she tried to lift her head.

Derek bent closer to the bed, studying the woman lying in it. She was small, her figure nearly lost beneath the sheets, and her eyes were wide and glassy. She was silent, though Derek could see her chest rising and falling rapidly in an uneven rhythm.

He reached out cautiously, his hand hovering over hers for a moment before finally making contact. Her skin was hot to the touch, and her body was trembling. A strange sense of dread settled upon him. He could feel her pulse racing beneath his fingertips.

Not knowing what he should do, he glanced around the room. There was no one else in sight, yet he couldn't shake the feeling that they weren't alone. His mind reeled with the questions that he wanted to ask.

With the contact, she began to mumble incoherently, thrashing about in the bed. Derek tried to remove his hand, not wanting to agitate her any further, but she wouldn't let go. At that moment, Father Mike returned with a nurse who turned off the distress monitor's screeching alarm. The nurse pried the old woman's fingers off Derek's arm and eased her back down into the bed.

Derek and Father Mike stood frozen in place as the old woman thrashed and muttered on the bed in front of them. The nurse rushed out of the room, saying something about the IV. It seemed like forever before she returned, clutching a vial in her hands. The nurse quickly inserted the contents of the vial into the old woman's IV. Suddenly, her ranting stopped and her body calmed. Derek and Father Mike let out a collective sigh of relief.

The nurse then carefully tucked the blanket around the old woman, her hands gently patting and smoothing the fabric. "There now," the nurse said softly, "everything is under control."

"Could you understand what she was saying?" Derek asked the nurse.

"Something about a granddaughter. She is very weak, and her heart is failing. If she had stayed in that agitated state, she would have expired. I had to sedate her to avoid any further damage to her heart." She cast them both a stern look. "You need to leave now."

It was only then that Derek and Father Mike truly noticed the profound silence that had descended on the room. The old woman was still, her eyes closed in a peaceful slumber. They could barely believe the change that had occurred in such a short amount of time. Their minds still reeling from the suddenness of it all, the two men proceeded to leave the room in silence.

They stopped at the sink before exiting the room to wash their hands. Then they walked down to the cafeteria to grab a cup of coffee and found a table in the corner.

"So, what was that all about?" Derek slid into a chair.

"She has a lot of demons fighting for her soul," Father Mike replied somberly. "When I come in, I rebuke them in the name of Jesus Christ. They come right back in to claim her because she is not saved and has been practicing witchcraft."

"What do you think she is trying to tell us about her granddaughter?" Derek wondered. "Has she mentioned her before?"

"No, this is the first time she has really become that animated." Father Mike took a sip of his coffee. "It appears she recognized you."

"She did. Maybe this has something to do with what happened to me."

Father Mike raised his eyebrows. "Possibly. It could all be linked in some way, but not in the way that you might think."

"Why?" Derek frowned. "What are you saying?"

The priest cradled his cup and took another sip. "You think she put a curse on you, right?"

"Well, yeah, it seems obvious, especially with what I just witnessed."

His mouth twisted. "Okay, you think these demons are living in you now and wrote all this on you?"

"Umm, I don't know. I think something like that could happen." Derek adjusted himself in the seat with a shrug. "So, what do you think?"

Father Mike answered in a firm voice. "I think you are giving the devil way too much power. I think this has more to do with you and your salvation and you being in a vulnerable place when you ran into her, than the devil having control over your body."

"So you don't think that something else did this to me?" Derek crossed his arms defensively. "You think I did this to myself?"

Other people had already told him essentially the same thing, including Dr. Cole, but it was still a bitter pill to swallow.

"I know that it is hard if not impossible for the devil to move in and take over a person's body without their permission," Father Mike said slowly. "I know that Jesus lives in your heart and when you accepted Jesus there were no demons that came up from inside of you—and believe me, they would have made themselves known once you proclaimed Jesus as your savior. They would not have been able to stay inside of you. These are things I do know. So, let's just take it from there."

Derek laced his fingers together, staring at the ink. "Okay, so if that is true then how did all this just appear on my skin overnight? There had to be something inside me for it to show up all over my skin like this."

Father Mike rested a hand on Derek's arm. "We will have to figure that out with the help of God."

"And how are we going to do that?" Derek leaned back, trying to keep his frustration in check.

"Through prayer, the Word and by helping this woman and anyone else that might need our help," Father Mike said calmly.

"How is helping everyone else going to solve *my* problem?"

Father Mike removed his hand from Derek's arm. "By loving your neighbor and treating them the way you would like to be treated. It will come."

Derek shook his head. "It sure seems like an indirect way to get there," he muttered.

"You said you have a Bible?" Father Mike held up his own in one hand.

"Yeah, I think so. Somewhere."

"Here, take this one." He handed the worn Bible to Derek. "Keep it close, start reading it. It may not make a whole lot of sense at first. But it will."

Derek had expected it to be heavier, but it surprisingly felt light in his hands. The leather cover was worn and the spine had been creased many times, indicating its history and importance.

Once back at the old woman's room, the men were informed there would be no more visitors per doctor's orders. They were forced to leave without answers.

"Remember," Father Mike said quietly. "No matter what, you are never alone." With that, he turned, leaving Derek with the Bible clutched to his chest.

Derek stood in the lobby of the hospital, tired and disappointed that he had not been able to get more information out of the old woman. After saying goodbye to Father Mike, he decided to take a seat for a few moments. He opened the Bible. Derek began to read, not quite sure what he was expecting, but feeling an inexplicable calm settle over his shoulders as he did so.

Chapter 7

Derek watched as Kendal's car sped away into the fog and disappeared. He stood frozen, the acrid scent of burnt rubber clinging to the air. Tears trickled down his face as he willed the car to come to a stop. But like a thunderstorm in the tropics, Kendal was gone in an instant, leaving Derek standing alone under a dark cloud . . .

He woke suddenly, his mind still entrenched in the raw sadness of the moment. As he took in his surroundings, he realized that he was in his bedroom. His skin was damp with cold sweat. He swung his legs over the side of the bed and padded quietly across the room to the window. He opened it, letting the chill night air fill the space, and breathed deeply, trying to shake off the heaviness that lingered in his heart.

Derek closed his eyes and pictures of Kendal flooded his mind. He remembered her smiling face, her infectious laughter, and the feel of her embrace. Then she fell from his arms and disappeared. Derek felt a crushing loss overtake him. He felt like he was starting to lose his mind.

He stumbled out of his bedroom, feet numb and heavy. Instinctively, he knew he had to keep going, that there was a purpose to this strange journey. The high moon illuminated his path as he walked slowly down the gravel driveway, feeling every crunch with a strange mix of anticipation and dread.

The night air felt thick and heavy in his lungs; the only sound was the chirping of crickets in the nearby bushes. He thought he could sense energy humming in the air, as if all the strange events of the past were converging toward this moment.

He was almost at the end of the driveway when he spied a figure standing in the shadows, barely visible in the moonlight. A chill rippled through his body. He stopped in his tracks and held his breath, unsure of what to do, as the figure slowly walked away. With a heavy heart and uneasy curiosity, he forced himself to take the first step toward the unknown.

Suddenly, the surroundings shifted and he was in a cemetery. He stopped in front of a headstone, reached out, and touched the cold, gray monument. He ran his fingers over the damp stone and felt a jolt at the realization that *Kendal Reed* was the name etched on the marker. The loss hit him once again.

Derek woke with a gasp to find he was still in bed. Had he just had a dream within a dream? Still unnerved, he rose and dressed in darkness, making his way down to the workout room, hoping exercise might banish the anxiety and confusion.

He started with cardio. Mounted a bike and began to pedal. He could still feel the remnants of his reaction to the dreams. He thought about what Dr. Cole would say.

He could hear her voice lecturing him: "Your dream confronts and exposes your flawed perspectives, and if you choose to ignore it then that means denying reality, which could stunt your progress and impede success."

I *am* learning to confront the truth, he told himself, no matter how difficult.

He had been told that doing so would help him reach his long-term objectives and goals and that's what he wanted to do. Little did he know that the dream was asking him to realize the mistakes of his thought process.

After a long, hard workout, he returned to his penthouse and stood in front of the massive wardrobe mirror. With his middle finger, he traced the perimeters of the tattoos. Following the lines slowly around his face and then down his neck, he etched the outline of the shield mounted on his right shoulder, stopping momentarily to examine the two swords and the dagger that crossed through the middle. He continued to his chest and then he saw it. A shudder ran through his body as he quickly lifted his finger from the winged serpent, recognizing the symbol of death. He instinctively knew that this tattoo represented destruction and evil.

It suddenly brought back another dream he'd recently had.

He was standing in the center of a clearing, transfixed by the sight before him. A massive, winged serpent, no less than twenty-five feet in length, coiled and contorted its body around a tall cypress tree. Its yellow eyes seemed to bore into his soul, and its forked tongue flickered menacingly, as if searching for its next victim.

He felt a chill snake down his spine, and he didn't dare move while he took in this strange and unsettling sight. What could the implications be of this winged serpent? The menacing feeling he felt just from looking at it couldn't be good.

Derek took a deep breath, then forced himself to slowly step forward. He crouched down behind a bush, determined to get a closer look at the creature. He was close enough now to see the serpent's scales glimmering in the fading light of the late afternoon sun. It was an impressive sight, one that made him feel both small and insignificant, yet simultaneously intrigued by the mystery of this winged beast.

The great beast turned its head to look down at Derek. He slowly stood up and began to back away from the serpent, when he felt a hand on his shoulder. Startled, he spun around to see Father Mike standing behind him.

"Don't be afraid," Father Mike said in a calming voice. "It's a guardian. It is here to protect this sacred space."

The priest's words brought some comfort to him, and he allowed himself to relax. But then he realized Father Mike would never tell him that a demonic figure would protect him.

The air around him shifted ever so slightly, and when he turned to look behind him, the figure he had thought was Father Mike had changed. His body language had shifted from familiarity to threat, and his face had turned into a demon's face. It was clear that the devil was doing everything he could to deceive him.

Derek knew he had to act fast. He reached into his pocket and felt for the crucifix. It was cold against his fingertips, a reminder of the power and protection it offered him against whatever machinations the devil had in store.

The figure stepped in closer, his eyes burning. "I'm here to offer you a deal," he said, voice thick with menace. "Your soul in exchange for your deepest desires."

Derek's heart skipped as he took a step back. He knew now that he was in a battle against something far darker and more powerful than anything he had encountered before. He could feel the awesome power radiating off the figure and he grasped his cross tightly, steeling himself for whatever came next . . .

With a shudder, he jerked back to the present. These dreams were so realistic. Looking at his reflection in the mirror, he wondered what was going to happen to him next. With trepidation, he turned quickly to inspect his back. He could see no further evidence of any other new tattoos or illustrations. Just the dark outlines of the existing tapestry, and bare virgin flesh in the center of his back where the faces of his childhood attackers once resided.

He would have to call Father Mike to see if he could help him figure out what these new dreams and new tattoos might mean. It was all so disturbing.

With an exhale of relief, he finished his examination and slowly stepped into the expansive shower to start his daily purgation.

He approached the daily-shower ritual in a synchronized order as he would prepare for surgery. Two adjustable mirrors hung in position for the sculpting of the front of the head, with one angled for the rear and the specific shaving utensils lined neatly on the shelf. Once the act of shaving was complete, he would scrub and inspect each tattoo.

Even though Kendal's shower had not been large enough to accommodate all the paraphernalia of his daily routine, he had perfected it while staying with her. Feeling the pangs of loneliness, he made his way through the methodical exercise.

The hand scrubber found its target and then moved with vigor while systematically analyzing each symbol. He patted down the fiery red illustrations with an oversized towel, stopping to inspect the new tattoo.

What could the implications of this winged serpent be? He definitely needed to call Father Mike to see if he had any explanation about the origin of the new tattoo.

He chose his usual outfit from the closet: a pair of jeans and a white V-neck T-shirt. He put the shirt and tie back in its place. Taking one last scrutinizing look in the mirror, he reluctantly made his way into the kitchen to start the coffee. He stood at the sliding glass door for a moment to watch Tyler's fluid movement as he held his pose on one leg and then crouched down. Derek whistled low and stepped back into the kitchen to retrieve his morning brew.

He opened the refrigerator, took out fresh fruit, and started cutting. Then he placed the cut fruit in small bowls and grabbed a couple of forks and two mugs off the rack. Not having a serving tray, he placed the items on a cutting board, opened the door, walked out quietly to the table, and set down the coffee and fruit.

Derek ate a forkful of fruit as he watched Tyler hold Sunrise pose.

He had made an important decision. Now, he just had to tell Kendal—it was going to be a difficult day. Feeling tired already from the anxiety, he took a sip of coffee. Then he breathed deeply, trying to absorb the energy and serenity of the space. Sitting motionless for a minute, he got up from the table and left for work.

When Derek arrived, the office was humming with activity. Surgeries had been booked for the morning, with both rooms filled. Derek walked past Nicole, the receptionist, not saying a word. He went straight back to his office and picked up the phone.

"Nicole."

"Yes, Dr. Hollinger?"

"Can you please send Kendal to my office?"

"Yes, doctor, as soon as she comes out of surgery."

"Thank you." Derek hung up the phone.

Looking through his schedule, he could see he had a few familiar names in the book. While he was making notes concerning the patients, Kendal entered.

"Good morning," she said with a bright smile, sitting down in one of the two large leather wingback chairs in front of his desk.

"Good morning." Derek stared back solemnly.

"What's going on?" She seemed to realize he wasn't dressed for work and looked vaguely alarmed.

"I've made some decisions."

"What kind of decisions?"

Unflinchingly, he answered, "Business decisions."

"Care to fill me in?"

"That's why I called you to my office."

"Okay?" She looked at him quizzically.

"I am going to have the partners take over my patient load."

Kendal sprang up like a shot. "Why in the world would you do that?" She leaned forward and braced her palms on his desk. "That's exactly what you have been trying to prevent!"

"Yeah, I know, but now I realize that it's inevitable and there's not a whole lot I can do about it. Not until I can get this—" he pointed to his face, "straightened out." He sat back in his chair.

Kendal threw her hands in the air. "So that's it. You're just giving up."

"No. Calm down." He was tired and didn't have the energy or desire to go toe-to-toe with her this morning.

"Don't tell me to calm down." Her cheeks were flushed with anger and disappointment. She strode to the door and rested one hand on the knob. "After everything that I've been doing to help you get through this, you just give up." Her eyes welled with tears. "You can't even try?"

"That's not what I am saying here." He slowly shook his head.

"Yeah, you are." A single tear slipped down her cheek. "You're saying you are just going to hand your business over to your partners."

Derek stood up from his chair. "Kendal, stop!"

"Stop what?" She swatted the tear from her face. "Telling you the truth?"

She spun on her heel and disappeared out the door.

Derek sank into his chair, swallowing an urge to lash out at the world. Then he got up and calmly walked down the hall to find her office empty. He proceeded to check both surgical rooms. Coming back to Nicole's desk, he asked, "Have you seen Kendal?"

"You just missed her." Nicole nodded toward the door.

Something told him to go out into the main hall. He looked both ways, then rushed to check the elevators, which were on separate floors. With multiple taps to the call button, the lights didn't illuminate to indicate that either one was on its way.

He dashed to the stairwell door and took the stairs down two at a time. Just as he hit the garage level, he saw her little red convertible pull out. Downshifting with a loud grind of gears, Kendal made the turn out of the parking garage, tires squealing. At that moment, a memory flash came, a déjà vu. He had experienced this scene before. As he stood there in the garage it came to him. This *was* his nightmare.

He ran for his motorcycle, turned the key, hit the button to start the engine, dropped the bike into gear and gave it the gas while releasing the clutch. The back tire started to fishtail as he kept his leg down, trying to keep the bike upright as his adrenaline spiked. He hit the street where the dip from the garage made the front wheel pop up as he flew through the first stop sign, and was almost taken out by a delivery truck.

Dodging other vehicles, he caught sight of the little red sports car. Twisting the throttle, Derek lay down on the tank. He knew instinctively this was a matter of life and death. At a center median that divided the street into four lanes, he caught up to Kendal.

"Pull over!" he yelled.

"No!" she screamed through her hot tears.

He honked his horn and put one hand over his heart. "Please!"

Her car slowed to a halt right before the four-way stop intersection. Suddenly, the sound of screeching tires came from a car that hit the curb and launched off the center island airborne over the hood of Kendal's car. It punched through a cinderblock wall, then disappeared. Derek jumped off his bike and pulled Kendal out of her car. "Are you all right?"

"Yes. Yes . . ." Her eyes were wide with amazement and shock.

Derek ran around the back of her car. "Call 911!" He jumped over what was left of the wall and vanished from sight.

Pulling her phone from her purse, Kendal followed. The car now sat perched with the back end straight up inside a swimming pool. Derek had jumped into the water trying to get the person out from behind the wheel. Kendal paced the side of the pool giving details to the 911 operator. Derek finally emerged from the water with an elderly man in his arms.

"Just hold on to him," Derek said, panting for breath.

Kendal had to lie on the ground to hold the man's arms and keep his head above water. Derek climbed out of the pool, grabbed the man under his arms, and carefully placed him on the concrete edge. Listening for his vitals, Derek began pushing hard on his chest and giving mouth-to-mouth resuscitation. He could hear the approaching sirens.

Kendal stood up and ran back out onto the street to flag them down. Within a minute the emergency crew came running up. Derek stepped aside to let the paramedics take over. He glanced up and his eyes widened, ice touching his spine.

The old shaman woman was watching from behind the sliding glass door inside the house. He quickly looked over at Kendal to grab her attention, but she was busy giving her statement. When he looked back, the shaman woman was gone like a mirage. In her place stood an Asian woman with no expression on her face. She closed the blinds.

He pulled himself together and turned his attention back to Kendal, walking over and giving her a big hug. "Are you okay?"

"Yes. I am now." She buried her head against his chest. Derek stroked her hair, shaken at how close he had come to losing the woman he loved.

Chapter 8

After giving their statements, Derek, who was still soaked, suggested they go back to his house for a change of clothes. Once they arrived, he motioned for Kendal to park her car next to his motorcycle inside his parking garage. He noticed that Tyler's bike was gone.

Upstairs in his penthouse, Kendal made herself at home while he went to change into some dry clothes. The kitchen was a grand display of modernity with polished hardwood floors, natural stone accents, and stainless-steel appliances. The large island, topped with sleek quartz countertops, dominated the space, but still begged to be used. Not a single pan or utensil graced the countertops, and the pantry shelves that lined the far side of the room looked as if they had been abandoned long ago.

The chairs, upholstered in rich leather and situated around a large dining table, sat empty and untouched. The only sign of life in the room was the faint hum of the refrigerator, a reminder that this was not a museum but a real, functioning home. Yet, it seemed as if the inhabitants had long since vanished, leaving behind this pristine, frozen moment. It made her feel sad. It had been three weeks since Kendal first let Derek come to stay in her apartment, and their constant bickering had only grown in intensity. She had watched as he walked out of the room, feeling her heart sink further and further with each step he took.

Yet she noticed a vase of fresh flowers on the windowsill. The vibrant colors and delicate petals brought a sense of warmth and life to the otherwise sterile space.

Kendal let out a deep sigh. Turning her attention back to the living room, she walked over to the bookshelf and ran a fingertip down the leather spines. She pulled out a couple and found that many of them were first-edition classics. She wondered as she looked at the titles how many Derek had actually read.

Suddenly, a tiny electric shock shot through her body. Startled, she drew in a deep breath and turned around to see him standing just a foot away, his tight white V-neck T-shirt replaced by a white button-down shirt.

The sight of him caused Kendal's heart to take a leap and the butterflies to come fluttering back into her stomach. She quickly put the book back up on the shelf and tried to compose herself. When she finally gathered the courage to look back up, Derek had already started to move away.

"What do you think?" he asked, a mischievous glint in his eye as he turned toward her with open arms. "Do I look better?"

She nodded.

Derek thought about the wine he had purchased just the day before. "Would you like a glass of wine to calm the nerves?"

Kendal nodded again. In the kitchen, he opened the first drawer and found it empty. He hadn't filled all the drawers yet. He knew instinctively that these empty drawers symbolized a lot of things. He stood for a moment in front of one of the drawers, letting his fingers graze the smooth wood as he contemplated the emptiness. They held significance for him; a representation of his past. The memories, the pain, the love—all packed away in these now vacant spaces. They were also a reminder of the choices he had made. But now, these empty drawers symbolized the future—an unknown and unpredictable future—waiting to be filled with endless possibilities.

Anything could happen, anything was possible. That thought filled him with excitement, fear and anxiety as he checked the next drawer and found it was empty, too. Then a third. At last, he found the wine opener with a sigh of relief. The last thing he needed was to appear disorganized. He handed Kendal her glass of wine as she stared out the kitchen window at his newly furnished balcony.

"Hey, would you like to check out my newest creation?" He opened the glass door and waved for her to go out onto the balcony.

Kendal's gaze swept the entire area. "It's beautiful."

"Really? You like it?" His face lit up.

"Like it?" She smiled back. "Oh, my goodness, I love it."

"It's not too much?" He ran over and pulled out a chair. "I didn't overdo it?"

"No, I think it's just right."

"I was a little worried about how many palm planters I put . . ." He scanned the balcony. "For the size of the balcony, but I thought if there were any less, then I wouldn't get the right feel, and if there were too many, well, then you know . . ." He realized he was babbling.

"It's just right, really I love it."

They locked eyes.

"Wow. Coming from you that really means a lot," he said in a low voice.

"What? You're crazy." She glanced away.

"I want to be able to relax when I come home. I didn't have that before. When I came back here it felt like I had returned to a sterile environment. It was still unfinished. I want it to be my happy place. A place that feels familiar, like your apartment, a home. I know a lot of it has to do with *you* being there, but some of it has to do with how you made it yours. When I walk in here, I want it to feel familiar. Do you know what I mean?"

"Yes, I do." She walked past him and looked out over the edge of the balcony, smiling as she thought about the contrast with her homey little apartment.

The ocean sparkled in the distance, a vast and endless expanse of water. She stood with the six-foot wall of glass behind her, the wind whipping her auburn hair with the sun's rays turning it into a dazzling display of sunburst. It was mesmerizing.

As Derek watched her, he felt a sense of peace wash over him. And in that moment, he knew that this was where he was meant to be, in this exact spot, at this exact time. But then he remembered his purpose. He took a deep breath. "Come have a seat." He motioned to the chair he was holding out. Derek waited for her to be seated and then sat down next to her.

"This is a great view," she gazed out into the distance.

"Yeah," he exhaled, "it is a great view."

They sat for a minute in silence sipping their wine.

"So, would you like to explain to me what is going on?" Kendal ventured.

"Well, things have been crazy the last couple of days. Terry called me and asked me to go to his shop to talk to a young man who needed some advice. It turns out it's an involved situation."

Kendal sat patiently listening.

"I decided to let the kid come home and spend a couple of days here to work things out."

"That's very kind of you." Kendal knew that by helping others it would help distract from his problems and negative self-talk.

"Well, we'll see about that." He rubbed his face. "Father Mike stopped by yesterday. He spent some time helping me to strengthen my faith. We discussed how I might overcome some of my recent life changes. During our conversation, he mentioned that he's trying to provide some spiritual guidance to an old woman who appears to be on her deathbed. I went to meet him at the hospital in San Diego last night. I do think it is the woman who put the curse on me."

"What?" Kendal jumped forward in her chair. "You found the old woman? Did she speak to you? Did she tell you why she put the curse on you?"

"No, she's in a coma. She fell and hit her head because she has a bad case of the flu."

"I'm so sorry." Kendal's shoulders slumped forward.

"After the day I had yesterday, I had more nightmares again last night. Then I found a new tattoo this morning."

"Oh no! Let me see it."

"It's on my chest."

Moving forward in her chair, she reached out to help him open his shirt. "Show me."

He quickly assisted Kendal unbuttoning his shirt. He stood and pointed to the winged serpent on his chest.

"Oh." She put her hand over her mouth.

"Yeah, believe it or not, this tattoo might be related to the reason I had to chase after you today."

"Why? What do you mean?"

"Well, I had a dream last night and then a premonition today. I knew I had to stop you or something bad was going to happen."

Kendal went pale. "Oh yeah, it would have been bad, all right. I would have been decapitated. That guy blew through that four-way stop. I would have been sitting at that stop sign right when he became airborne, he would have hit me right smack at head level. It wouldn't have been pretty." She shivered and hugged herself. "Thank God, I had you there."

"And that's what's starting to scare me. What if I hadn't gotten to you in time?"

"Well, thank God, we don't have to think about that."

"Maybe this time, but what about next time?" He put his hands in his back pockets.

It wasn't lost on Kendal that the pose showed off his toned physique. "Don't say that. Oh, my goodness."

"I had bad dreams last night." He sat back down at the table. "The new tattoo appeared this morning, and then this premonition."

"Do you think any of this has to do with seeing the old woman again?

"Possibly. I think I saw her at the accident site, too."

Kendal flinched. "What do you mean?"

"She stood at the sliding glass door of the house, peering out at us." He thought back to how her wrinkled face seemed to be illuminated.

Kendal's heart started to race.

"I think she might have the power to become a spirit." He felt a shiver run down his spine as their eyes met. "When I turned to grab your attention, you were talking with the police. I looked back, and the shaman woman was gone. It was like she had been a mirage. In her place stood an Asian woman with jet-black hair and no expression on her face. Then she closed the blinds on the sliding glass door."

Kendal's mind raced with questions. *Was the shaman woman real or a figment of his imagination?*

"I can't shake off the feeling that something strange is happening."

They both sat quiet, deep in thought until Derek decided to change the subject. "The talk I had with Father Mike got serious."

"About what?" Kendal asked.

"We discussed my faith and the status of my soul."

"That does sound serious."

"Now these things are happening and I'm not sure how it is all related."

"Well, maybe you should go back to the beginning of the day." Kendal shot him a look. "You started by telling me that you are going to hand the business over to the partners."

"I'm *not handing* the business over to the partners. I am going to make a deal with them to run the practice until I can get back on my feet. I can't let it just flounder and die. I don't know if these unexpected changes are going to continue. It creates significant stress. It throws me into an emotional spiral and affects my judgment, especially while performing surgery. People don't have confidence in me."

"Come on, that's not true."

"Sure, it is. You don't have confidence in me. It affects my decision-making process. My feelings of anxiety and depression flare up. Be realistic. I can't take it personally. All I need to do is put myself in your place. The shoe doesn't fit anymore, then kick it off, right?"

She set her wine down. "Okay, then if you're not planning on coming into work anymore, what are you going to do?"

"Well, for one thing, Father Mike needs help at his clinic. I'm going to see what I can do for the people he serves. I'll still have to use our facilities at times."

"That's a great idea." She brightened. "I love that. Is there anything I can do?"

"Probably, but I need to see how it's all going to work. In the meantime, I need to get back down to San Diego to talk to the old woman. She's in pretty bad shape."

"Do you think she'll wake from her coma?"

"They don't know. She fell and hit her head because she was so weak. Father Mike believes she came from deep in the Amazon, they've probably had minimal exposure to these types of viruses. They don't expect her to make it. She's barely hanging on. Her lungs are filled with fluid and she's in heart failure."

"Oh, no, I am so sorry. It sounds like you need to get back to the hospital as soon as possible."

"Father Mike and I are waiting for the doctor to give us permission to go back in. She got pretty agitated at our last visit."

"She woke up while you were there? Do you think she recognized you and that's why the new tattoo came up?" Kendal wanted to reach out to run her fingers over the smooth serpent.

"After what happened today, I'm thinking, it might be some sort of warning."

"A warning for what?"

He shook his head in frustration. "I haven't been able to connect the dots. But what happened today might be linked to one of these tattoos. Since I've learned some of the possible meanings, I believe there might be a message here, telegraphed by my emotions. Look what happened when we first got together. The chains came off and the rose turned red. So, there must be some connection between what I'm experiencing and what these things represent."

"That's right, I wasn't thinking about that." Kendal brought her attention to the rose on his chest, stroking it gently.

He grabbed the palm of her hand and started kissing it.

The butterflies fluttered as she closed her eyes. He pulled her forward onto his lap as he started to slowly kiss her neck. She could feel the warmth of his mouth and smell his scent as she grabbed the back of his head to pull him forward and press her lips to his. Her passion rose, but the voice of reason piped up and she pulled away. "We can't do this."

"Do what?" Derek was confused.

"Start back up and become intimate like everything is okay between us."

"I don't get it. What do you want from me?" He slammed back into his chair.

"That's just it! Until you can figure that part out, I can't be with you. All you know how to do is be *about you* and I need someone who is going to be there for *me*."

"What are you talking about? I ran after you today to make sure you didn't end up in some crazy accident." His brow furrowed. "I think that shows that I am looking out for you."

"Yes, and I appreciate that. But there is a lot more to a relationship than a premonition."

"Why did you come home with me?" He buttoned his shirt back up.

"To find out what's going on. Just because we can't have an intimate relationship doesn't mean I don't care what happens."

"Oh, please, you ran out of the office today like your hair was on fire."

"I'm upset. The partners know how close you and I are—they might decide they don't want me around."

"That's not how it's going to play out. I am working a deal to make sure that they're happy."

"How do you know they'll accept?"

"The offer comes bearing gifts, mainly money and fame. Who wouldn't?"

Kendal gave him a level look. "Okay, so where does that leave me?"

"Where do you want it to leave you?"

"Obviously, I'll have a lot of responsibility to make sure that things are maintained at their current levels, correct?"

"Yes, that is what I am hoping for."

"Okay, then I want a part of the action."

His brows rose. "Wow, I didn't see that coming."

"Why not? I've been the one to stabilize the business."

Derek sighed. "Okay, what are we talking about here?"

She jutted her chin out. "Ten percent."

"That's not going to happen." He shook his head.

"Okay, then what do you think?"

"Three percent on top of what you are getting right now. That is one percent for each one of us. It keeps your finger in the pie."

"No, that's not enough."

"Okay, after five years it will go to five percent and after ten years it will cap at ten percent divided by the three partners, and we all have to agree. So, I will have to have an agreement drawn."

She gave a satisfied nod. "That works."

Derek scowled. "I feel like my bones have just been picked clean."

"Now you know how I feel all the time when decisions are being made without any consideration for my thoughts or hard work."

"Okay, are we done?" He pushed up from the chair.

"I believe we are." She turned to leave.

"Let me walk you out."

Kendal felt the sting of Derek's dismissal but knew she had to take the opportunity to protect herself before the upcoming meeting. She also knew that their relationship was not at a point where it could move forward—*if* it could move forward. She reluctantly picked up her things and left.

Tyler pulled into the parking slot right behind the little red sports car pulling out. He found Derek at the table on the deck.

"Hey, how are you? What's going on?" Derek asked Tyler as he came walking out to the balcony.

"I talked to Terry," he sat down in a chair and spoke firmly, "and we are going to meet with these guys tonight."

"Why in the world would you want to do that?"

"To see if we can negotiate." Tyler made eye contact.

"Negotiate what? You already know what they want."

His eyes softened. "Yes, that's true but they may want something more. Until we talk, I won't know what that is."

"Okay, I see your point." Derek made a move to stand up. "I'll go with you."

Tyler raised a hand. "No, I don't think that would be a good idea."

Derek sat back down on the edge of his chair. "Of course, it is. I'm here to back you up."

"You have your own stuff going on. You don't need to get into this mess."

"Well, put it this way, I am waiting for a call from the hospital, as soon as I get that call, I am heading back down to San Diego. Until then, I am all yours."

"Okay, that sounds fair." Tyler rubbed his hands together. "I really appreciate the help."

"So, what's the plan?" Derek relaxed back into his seat.

"Well, Terry found out who these guys are and where they hang out. He's getting his men together and we're going to meet, then go over there tonight."

"So, you are going to have a showdown." He leaned forward, elbows on his knees.

"Yeah, something like that." Tyler looked down at his hands.

"Okay, so what are your terms going to be?" Derek watched Tyler's expression to see if he had thought this out.

"I am going to see if my brother is there and if I can get any information on where they are keeping him—or at least find out if there is any way of negotiating other terms."

"So," Derek gave a dry chuckle, "we're just going to ride in on the seat of our pants and hope for the best."

"Well, what do you propose?"

"A strategy," Derek leaned in, "you need to have a strategy."

"Okay, I am down with that."

"We need to think this through. What are they going to gain by having you fight?"

"I assume they expect to make a lot of money."

"Okay, how?"

"By betting on me, or against me, I'm not sure yet. But right now, I would think it is on me, because of the magical tattoos."

Derek cocked his head and shrugged his shoulders. "Or it could be against you, the odds are going to be a lot higher if you lose. They are going to hype you up and everyone is going to be betting on your magical tattoos. They may want you to take a fall."

"That's true if they only want a one-time fight."

"I would have to guess that this is a one-time shot because they can't keep your brother forever and that makes this very dangerous."

"Maybe." Tyler nodded.

"So, who are the guys they are going to be dealing with that they are going to double-cross?" Derek asked.

"Wow, that's a good question."

"I think we need to talk to Terry." Derek stood. "Let's take a ride."

Chapter 9

The tavern door opened, and a burst of light illuminated the dimly lit bar. Terry turned on his barstool, squinting to make out the silhouettes of two men who had paused momentarily to adjust to the sudden light. The thud of the door closing behind them signaled the return of darkness and the end of their hesitation.

"Doc, over here!" Terry yelled, recognizing one of the figures as Derek.

The two men stepped forward into the pool of soft light coming from the dim fixtures hanging from the ceiling behind the bar.

"Hey Doc, how are you?" Terry inquired, as he motioned for the men, whom he had been holding court with, to move further down the bar.

Tyler edged up to the barstool next to Terry.

Terry studied Tyler's face. A quiet, introspective young man, but this evening his demeanor seemed even more subdued than he had been earlier that day, as if he were carrying some secret burden.

"I've been better." Derek took his seat at the barstool next to Tyler and quietly ordered a beer. Tyler declined with a wave of his hand. "What did you find out?"

Terry removed the cigar from his mouth. "This is a serious group."

"How is that?" Derek asked as he leaned on the bar, looking past

Tyler to move in closer to hear the conversation over the jukebox music.

"These guys have their hands in all kinds of stuff," Terry growled.

"That figures." Derek shook his head.

"They're really just small-time, but the guys they're connected to get pretty serious," Terry continued.

"Who are they?" Tyler asked.

"Well, according to my sources at the LAPD, these guys are just a small-time street gang. The head of the snake is an organized crime ring out of Chicago. The FBI and the Chicago police have been watching them for a while. I found out where their 'Tong' or meeting hall is located. This fraternal organization is having its weekly gathering tonight. We can stake out the meeting hall where they discuss their illegal activities, then follow them back to their place. This will hopefully lead us to Tyler's brother."

"They have weekly meetings?" Derek asked.

"Yes, they're very organized. They launder large amounts of money from their illicit activities through Asian banks and businesses. They're connected directly to China. They have criminal organizations set up for money laundering, illegal gambling, counterfeiting, theft of computer software, and human trafficking, and that's just to name a few."

Tyler leaned in, "So, these guys are the Chinese Mafia, essentially."

"Yeah, it looks like it." Terry forced the air through his vocal cords to release a froglike voice. "They're ruthless. Some of them are violent criminals with ancient ethnic hostilities that can erupt into gang warfare and mayhem at the drop of a hat. So, we should really be careful.

"Their main product is fentanyl, otherwise known as Apache,

China Girl, China Town, Dance Fever, and TNT. Lots of other names, but I can't remember them all. It's a synthetic opioid about a hundred times more potent than morphine and fifty times more potent than heroin.

"My guys down at the police department tell me fentanyl-laced drugs are extremely dangerous when taken with other substances, particularly alcohol or illicit drugs such as heroin or cocaine, and can cause respiratory distress and even death. These thugs are going to be heavily armed with semi-automatic weapons. They've already been involved in several shootouts this past year."

"With whom?" Derek took a sip of his beer.

"With the LAPD. When I spoke to the police about the MMA fighting, they said they hadn't heard about it. So this must be a new business venture." He took a sip of his beer.

"Okay, so maybe the big boys aren't involved yet." Derek twisted his lips to one side, biting the lower lip with the thought that maybe these guys might be going rogue.

"I can't imagine that these guys are smart enough to do anything on their own," Terry said. "The big guys will be involved at some point. There's too much money at stake."

Terry eyed the two men with curiosity, sensing that they might be ready for an adventure. "Do you two want to join me on a little journey tonight?" he asked, a hint of excitement in his voice. His suspicions were confirmed when Derek and Tyler exchanged a glance before nodding in unison. Derek smiled and gestured for the bartender to bring him another beer. The night had just begun.

Terry's voice vibrated, "We have to find out how all the pieces fit. I think only a couple of us should go stake out the place, not to draw attention. The rest can wait a couple of blocks away, as backup. Then once we get a tail on them, we can let you know where we are heading."

"I have an idea," Tyler said. "How about if I put a GPS app locator on our phones and we can all coordinate?"

"Perfect. Let's do that," Terry agreed, summoning his buddies. "Hey, guys come over here, give me your phones."

Terry and Tyler sat across the street, behind a dumpster, in an old pickup truck, watching the line of vehicles fill the restaurant parking lot. Two large Asian guards were stationed at the entrance to open the door of each limousine that pulled into the parking lot to deposit dark-suited men. They climbed the steps to receive a quick pat-down before entering the establishment.

There was little movement for a couple of hours. Then the door opened, and the stream of suits piled back into their limousines. The line of vehicles started to drain from the parking lot.

Tyler's heart raced. "That's them. Those are the guys that took my brother."

"Okay, good," Terry said in a hushed voice.

The men sat in the backseat of a Lincoln Continental as they drove past. Terry and Tyler crouched low in the cab of their pickup, then texted Derek to alert him that they were in pursuit. This was the signal that they would be passing his location shortly.

The Lincoln Continental came to a stop at the first light. Terry slowed. When the car made a turn, their old pickup truck went straight, and Derek picked up the pursuit in Terry's old, rusty Volkswagen van from the opposite direction.

Derek made sure he stayed a few car lengths back so there would be no eye contact. The next turn was residential. Derek passed the street, then Terry's boys came in a couple of seconds later from an alternate street. An address was texted out to everyone. Derek parked on a side street and jumped into the truck with Terry and Tyler. Terry's men sat staking out the house from a couple of houses away.

They drove up to a house that was a shell of its former self, with peeling paint and broken shutters. The windows were covered in tattered curtains, their faded floral patterns barely recognizable.

The three men approached the house cautiously. Derek took the lead, knocking on the door. Heavy footsteps sounded. A big man with a gun in his waistband swung the door back and stood staring at the three men standing on the landing in front of him.

"I need to speak to your boss," Derek said.

"Who's asking?" the big man inquired.

"I have a business proposition for him."

"Who are you?"

"Just tell him a potential business associate."

The door slammed shut and the three stood in silence. After a minute, the door swung back open, and the man stepped aside, motioning for them to enter. Derek stepped in cautiously, while Tyler followed with Terry bringing up the rear. The floorboards creaked beneath their weight as they made their way through the dusty hallway.

They followed the large man through the hallway out into a living room where a half-dozen people milled around drinking and smoking miniature glass pipes. The walls were bare, stripped of any decorations or photographs that may have once adorned them. The house felt lifeless, a sad reminder of what once was.

A young Asian man entered the room. His eyes widened upon seeing three men, one with tattoos covering his face and bald head. "What's your business here, Tatman?" he asked, sinking into a large wingback chair without breaking his glare.

Derek stood tall with his legs apart. "I'm here to ask you to give us my friend's brother."

"Why would I do that?" he asked, looking directly at Tyler.

"I know there's something you want." Derek took a step forward. "And it's more than just one fight. I'm wondering how much of a cut your bosses are receiving?"

"What?" In a single blurring motion, he pulled a gun and pointed it straight at Derek's forehead.

"One fight." Derek kept his voice level. "We keep our mouths shut, you keep your money, and he gets his brother back."

The man waved the gun. "What about all the money his brother owes me?"

"That's why I'm here." Tyler stepped forward.

Derek put his hand on Tyler's chest.

"No," the gangster said. "You're fighting to keep his ass alive. He still owes me a hundred grand for a boatload of China Girl." He aimed the gun at Tyler.

Tyler started to take a step forward. The click of the hammer cocking stopped him. "Your guys said it was a gambling debt," he protested.

"It is a gambling debt." He waved the gun. "He took my drugs. Now he's gambling with his life." He chuckled at his own words.

"I can't pay that kind of money," Tyler objected.

"Wait." Derek raised his hands. "We'll give you a hundred grand, but only after we have his brother in our custody after the fight—win, lose, or draw."

The gun swung back to Derek. "No, he has to win, or the kid is dead."

"Then you don't get your money for the fight or the kid." Derek put his hands back down.

"Then the kid is dead, period." He released the hammer and waved the gun. "Now, get out of here; quit wasting my time."

The big guy grabbed Tyler by the arm. Tyler quickly swung his arm downward to break free from his grip, then brought him down to the floor.

The gangster smirked. "Nice move, but the guys you are going to be up against Friday night aren't going to be as big and dumb as my gorilla here."

"Come on let's get out of here," Derek said as he wrenched Tyler off the guy on the ground, while Terry kept an eye on the man with the gun. No one else in the room seemed to be paying the altercation any attention.

When the three reached their truck, Terry motioned for his men to go back to the bar.

"He didn't seem too intimidated waving that gun around. What do you have on him?" Tyler asked climbing into the truck cab first, seated in the middle.

"Oh, I think he might be just a little more worried than he let on. He knows if this gets out, he is going to be in some deep trouble with the big guys. He's going to play it cool, so we can't strong-arm him. This is just the beginning, watch." Terry started the truck.

Tyler chewed his lip with a worried frown. "Do you think he'll do something to my brother for us trying to threaten him?"

"If they were going to do something, they would have already done it." Derek lowered the brim of his cap to shield his eyes from the sun.

"You think they've hurt or killed him, or something?" Tyler looked over at Terry.

"No, they're not going to start torturing him just because we showed up. I think they're holding him someplace until after the fight." Terry stared through the windshield at the road ahead.

Derek leaned forward to look at Tyler. "Do you have any idea what your competition is looking like?"

Tyler met his gaze. "Yes, I went online and checked out some of the fighters, most of them are local. There's only one who comes out of Thailand. I'm hoping he's taken out before we come up against each other."

"How many matches do you have to fight?" Derek asked.

Tyler shrugged. "One, maybe two."

"Have they already put your name in?" Derek looked out the side window.

"Yes, they already have all my information posted online. I guess my brother gave it to them." He looked glum. "I'll be known as Magic Monk."

"You are doing this to save a life, remember?" Derek tried to reinforce Tyler's decision.

Tyler sat composed yet weary, his hands resting on his lap. "There is never a good reason to use these tattoos to bring harm to others," he began, his voice strong yet tinged with sadness. "I understand the responsibility that comes with it, and I must always use them for the greater good."

"But sometimes there are no other options. This is to save someone and to defend yourself, so I believe you are justified in your actions." Derek pulled out his cellphone. "Listen, I'll meet you back at the penthouse. I have to go back down to San Diego. We just got the okay to go back in and see the old lady."

Terry flashed a look his way. "Do you think she has some information for you?"

"I hope so," Derek rubbed his chin. "I believe she knows something. I'm just not sure what it could be."

Terry pulled over. Derek opened the door and climbed out.

"Well, I hope she can shed some light on it for you." With a raspy breath, Terry exhaled, "Good luck."

Chapter 10

Derek dropped off the van in the Tremendous Tattoos parking lot, then mounted his motorcycle, which was parked next to Tyler's. By the time he arrived at the hospital, visiting hours were over, and the halls were quiet. He found Father Mike praying at the old woman's bedside. He waited in the doorway until the priest made the sign of the cross and motioned for Derek to come into the room.

"She's still not awake. She's been resting soundly, but no change in her condition. Her vitals have been stable since yesterday."

Derek nodded from behind his mask. He gazed at the frail old woman lying motionless under the sheets, wondering yet again what the connection between them could be.

Father Mike edged his way around the bed. "I'm going out to talk to the nurse, but I'll be back."

Derek moved to the threshold of the bed, hesitant. The old woman lay inanimate, her skin a parchment of wrinkles and blemishes, a life written in deep creases and hollows. He'd never seen a person lie so still, so silent, except under sedation. It was as if she'd been barely breathing in a state of suspended animation.

He moved in closer and sat down next to the bed, his eyes drawn to the intricately inked markings on the woman's face. He lifted the sheet to look at her arms and hands, searching for any evidence of further markings.

Gently placing the sheet back down, he glanced at the side table. The first thing he noticed was a little wooden figurine. Cupping it in his hands, he studied the detailed carvings and read the two simple letters etched on the bottom: "DH."

Derek's vision started to blur as the blood rushed to his head. Memories of his own grandmother came flooding back. It was the last day of his freshman year in high school. He was supposed to walk home after school. His mom had made arrangements with Carol, his grandmother, to have her come out to visit. She was going to be flying into town that day. He had to get home to go with his mom to pick her up. He had tried to get out of it, but his mom insisted he be with her at the airport when his grandmother arrived.

Carol and her grandson had always been close, especially after her son's passing. They would often spend hours together, with Derek listening intently as she shared stories and passages from the Bible. Through their shared grief for the loss of his father, they had formed an unbreakable bond.

In woodshop class, he had crafted a small wooden figure of an angel as a tribute to his late father. He was certain that his grandmother would hold it dear.

When Derek was brought out of the coma, his mother, Sandi, made the decision not to inform him of his grandmother's passing. He had no recollection of her being present during his coma.

Eventually, he recalled the reason for being on that sidewalk on that fateful day. The details of his grandmother's passing also came back to him. The memories only fueled his anger and resentment toward his mother. He held her responsible for the traumatic events that unfolded due to her decisions. His hostile emotions were confirmed by the few memories that remained. The traumatic experiences that plagued him in his sleep were a result of choices made by his mother. He held her responsible for his lost high school years and the passing of his beloved grandmother.

As Derek gently set the figurine on the nightstand, he rose to his feet with a sense of nostalgia that seemed to stretch back an eternity. Father Mike's voice sounded far away as he felt himself drifting into unconsciousness. He took a few steps backward, taking in the surreal feeling of being present yet so distant from everything around him. His grip on consciousness was slipping, and the last thing he heard was Father Mike's voice echoing in the room before everything went dark.

When Derek regained consciousness, he found himself seated in a wheelchair in the hallway outside the old woman's room. A nurse stood on one side, her face grim. On the other side was Father Mike, looking concerned.

Derek tried to focus on his surroundings—the nurse's pristine uniform, the smell of antiseptics, the bright fluorescent lights that lined the hall. He felt as though he had been in a deep sleep, and as he slowly came to, a sudden realization dawned on him. He had intuitively been summoned here, but why?

"Are you okay?" Father Mike asked.

"What happened?" He looked down at the cuff on his arm, then over at the nurse taking his blood pressure. "Padre, the wooden angel on her nightstand—"

"Yes, I saw it there this morning."

"Where did it come from?"

"I'm not sure. Have you seen it before?"

"Yes. I made it when I was in high school. A gift for my grandmother right before I was attacked. After that, I never saw it again."

"How do you know this is your angel?"

"Go get it, please."

Father Mike walked back into the room and came out with the little wooden angel in the palm of his hand.

"Look on the bottom."

Father Mike looked closely at the bottom of the angel. "It says D.H."

"That's me. Derek Hollinger. I put my initials on it when I finished. It was a school project. I made it for my grandmother. I had put it in my backpack to take home. I'd forgotten all about it until I saw it sitting on the side of her bed. Then it all came back to me. They stole my backpack and my dad's baseball cap right off my head."

Father Mike handed the little wooden figurine back over to Derek as the nurse finished taking his pulse.

"How are you feeling now, Mr. Hollinger?" the nurse asked.

"Dr. Hollinger," Father Mike corrected.

"Oh." The nurse looked into his tattooed face and dropped the stethoscope into his lap. "I am so sorry, Dr. Hollinger, please forgive me. I didn't know."

"Don't worry about it. You're not the first person to be surprised," Derek said as he handed the instrument back to the nurse. "Do you know where this figurine came from that was on the old lady's side table?"

"No, doctor, I don't, but I can ask the morning nurse and find out."

"Please, this is very important to me."

The nurse turned quickly and left.

"This is too bizarre. How in the world could this all be linked?" Derek wondered.

"Well, we know there is a connection here someplace." Father Mike stood in the door of the shaman's room looking in.

"Yes. And it's hopefully going to lead right back to these tattoos."

"God willing," Father Mike added.

The nurse came back with a smile on her face. "It was given to her by the patient in the room next door when he left."

"Who was the patient?"

"I don't know, I didn't ask. I can find out for you." The nurse stood with her hands clasped in front of her waist.

"Please, find out for me and give him a call and ask him where he got the figurine, if you would, please. Thank you."

The men went back into the hospital room, while the nurse went to see if she could track down the origin of the figurine.

Father Mike stood by the patient, who lay in a quiet state of unconsciousness. "Maybe we should take turns sitting with her. Are you going to be okay?"

"Yes. I am better now. That's a great idea. I would like to take the first shift if that is all right with you," Derek suggested.

Father Mike put his hand on Derek's shoulder. Derek shook his head, unsure how to put the feelings swirling inside him into words. He hated having to come to this place. He felt like it was trying to suffocate him.

Father Mike looked at him with caring eyes. "Of course, but do you feel okay?"

His hand rested on Derek's shoulder, and the warmth of the gesture was almost too much for Derek to bear. He wanted to tell him everything, the fearful feeling of not having control—but he couldn't. He had to be strong. Instead, he simply nodded and gave a small smile of reassurance that he didn't feel.

"Yes, really, I'm okay," he said. "I just needed a minute, that's all."

Father Mike smiled back, understanding that Derek wasn't ready to open up yet about what he had just experienced. "That's why I'm here," he said gently. "Whenever you're ready to talk, I'm here to listen.

"I should make some rounds and see some other patients," he said in a low voice, "I'll be back a little later."

The room was dark—the only sound, the familiar but somber beeping of the machinery monitoring the life of the motionless old woman. Sitting in the chair next to her bed, Derek remembered how he had whittled the tiny angel all those years ago, the same one that he had carefully wrapped and put into the pocket of his backpack.

He remembered the days of sitting in the sun in the park, and the conversations with his grandmother while they fed the ducks and watched the birds flutter past.

And yet, for some reason, Derek had not remembered the angel when he finally got his memories back from before that awful day. Why had he forgotten the angel? A sharp pain of guilt and regret stabbed his chest as he sat there looking at the woman before him, feeling a mixture of profound sorrow and love for the grandmother he had lost and had never had the opportunity to mourn.

The day he was attacked, and his grandmother was coming to visit, Derek had wanted to see her—but it was the last day of school, the start of summer vacation, and he'd secretly been resentful, wishing he could hang out with his friends instead.

So after the bell rang at school, he'd stalled for as long as he could, hoping to wiggle out of picking his grandmother up at the airport. By the time he started for home, the school grounds were empty of kids, the surrounding streets largely deserted.

He was slowly walking home when a car screeched to a stop in front of him. A bunch of men jumped out—all older and quite a bit bigger than Derek. They had shaved heads with tattoos and piercings. The ringleader had a tattoo of a spider web that circled the left side of his face.

He was terrified and tried to run, but the gang caught him before he took three steps. When his mother found him bleeding on the sidewalk an hour later, Derek was unconscious and nearly dead, with severe head trauma and a dozen broken bones.

His recovery took years. He missed the rest of high school, and lost all his friends and everything that mattered to him.

But the tragedy didn't end there. The shock of learning about the assault gave his grandmother a heart attack right at the hospital. Derek never saw her again.

In his secret heart, he blamed himself for all of it. If he had just done as his mother asked and gone straight home, he never would have run into the gang, and his grandmother might still be alive.

When he crossed paths with Spider all these years later outside Father Mike's revival tent, Derek learned that the attack was random. Just a horrible twist of fate . . .

He dragged himself back to the present as the nurse came into the room.

In a low voice she said, "The patient's roommate gave it to him right before he passed away. The roommate told him that the angel had been the only good thing he had possessed in his life. So, when the patient was healed suddenly, he attributed it to the angel. He felt compelled to give it to this sick old lady who had the room next door as he was leaving the hospital."

Derek's pulse raced. "Can you find out who his roommate was who passed away, please?"

"I can try." She frowned slightly. "But the hospital doesn't like us to give out that kind of information unless you are on staff."

"I really *am* a doctor," he said, pulling out his wallet and showing her his identification. "Ah, this is for a case I'm working on with Father Mike."

Her demeanor changed immediately. "Yes, doctor."

The nurse turned and left the room. Derek opened the blinds to look out the window; for a moment, he could almost forget where he was. The wind rustled the trees outside, and a flock of blackbirds flew across the night sky. He closed his eyes and was at once filled with an overwhelming sense of peace.

He slouched back into the chair, the weight of exhaustion pressing down on him, and allowed his eyelids to slip closed. Just a quick rest . . .

Derek opened his eyes to find the hospital room cloaked in a soft, gray fog. The air felt warm and heavy, and a strange scent hung in the air. He blinked several times, but the fog was still there. He had been dreaming, and he realized he was *still* dreaming.

Suddenly, a figure appeared out of the fog. It was the old shaman woman, her gray hair and her network of wrinkles a testament to an eternity of life's lessons.

"Where are we?" he asked, confused.

With an air of mystery, the old woman spoke. "Somewhere between your subconscious mind and your conscious mind."

"You speak my language," he said.

"You speak *my* language." She smiled.

"Why did you do this to me?" Derek's mind was filled with uncertainty.

"Do you believe in the power of good and evil?"

Derek paused to consider the question. He believed that there was a balance between them, but he had never experienced anything like this before. He wasn't sure how to answer.

Suddenly, he was overcome with a strange feeling. It was as if he were being pulled toward something—something deep and powerful. What was it that was calling him? He didn't know. All he knew was that he had to find out.

"My people believe that when you suffer a trauma," she said, "a piece of your soul flees your body in order to survive the experience. Do you remember your soul leaving your body right after you were beaten?"

He closed his eyes, a chill touching his spine. "I do remember the moment when I knew that my soul had left my body. When that stick had struck my head. I woke up a very different person. It was a feeling like none other, a realization that something integral to me had gone away. I felt a sudden, sweeping emptiness in the core of my being."

For the first time in weeks, Derek's mind felt clear. He saw the truth that had been hidden for so long. "The trauma had been too much for me to bear, and so my soul fled. I was lucky to have survived the encounter with the men who had beaten me so brutally, but I was also at a loss for why my soul had left. I remember asking myself what would happen if my soul didn't return. If it was lost forever."

He thought for a second about the bond between his soul and his body, and how deeply they were intertwined. "As I lay there, battered, with my bones broken, I remember feeling a warmth in my chest that had spread throughout my body. Slowly, I began to sense my soul's return and knew I had to keep living.

"I have come to believe that our souls are stronger than we realize. Even in the most dire of circumstances, they cling to our bodies, and will never abandon us completely until the final day. But on that fateful day, my soul and I shared a moment of profound understanding. It had left me in order to survive, but it did come back."

He looked into her dark, wise eyes. "And I am grateful for its return. Thanks to this strength that it gave me for the will to live, I am alive today."

The old woman opened her arms. "The soul goes into the sixth dimension. I met you there. I was looking for access to someone. The whole soul sometimes doesn't come back on its own, leaving it vulnerable. Fragmented. Traditionally, in my village, it is customary for me to go to the sixth dimension, the final realm, the highest place of existence.

"There, I am beyond time, capable of doing things beyond imagination. It is a place where I can influence and control nature, track down the fractured soul and return the missing piece to the owner's body. I can do this for you. But I am here to ask that you return the favor and do something for me."

"How do the tattoos come into all of this?" Derek felt more confused than ever.

"Find my granddaughter." She disappeared back into the fog.

Derek woke from the vision as the nurse walked into the room. He drew a steadying breath.

"Dr. Hollinger," she said, "I have the name of the man who gave the figurine to the patient next door."

Derek felt a massive weight bearing down on him; he already knew the answer but needed to be certain.

"What's the name?" he asked, not looking up at her.

"It's very weird." She glanced at her clipboard. "I've never seen this before. No proper name is listed, first or last. We only have the name *Spider*."

Chapter 11

Derek returned to his penthouse at a little past midnight, his brain scrambled from the day's events. The shaman woman seemed to be somehow linked to Spider. Thanks to a series of strange coincidences, she'd ended up with the angel figurine he had whittled for his grandmother. What was the connection between them? How did his tattoos fit into it all?

He had been given one more piece of the puzzle. Another clue. Yet he found himself with more questions than ever.

When Derek opened the door, Tyler was waiting.

"Hey Doc," he said eagerly, "did you find out anything?"

"Yes and no. It was another crazy night." Derek fell onto his chair.

"I've been thinking, I'm still not sure fighting is the best way to handle this." Tyler stood in front of Derek, oblivious to his exhaustion. "What if I lose and I never see my brother again? What if I win and they decide to keep my brother and make me fight again?"

After his night at the hospital, Tyler's problems were almost too much for Derek to process, but he'd offered to help the kid and wouldn't abandon him now. "That's why I'm using the 'boss card,'" Derek muttered wearily.

"I don't understand." Tyler sank down in the next chair. "What information do you have that will make them back down?"

"Terry is still digging." He paused to find the energy to explain. "It appears that they are up to some fight-club type racketeering. We have a hunch this latest criminal activity may become a way for them to earn a nice chunk of illegal money on the side."

Derek sighed. "I'm pretty sure that the big bosses don't know anything about it. And if that is true, then they're dead men. So, that's our ace in the hole."

"And Terry is working on this ace in the hole?" Tyler persisted.

"Yes, he has a lot of connections down at the LAPD," Derek reassured him. "They've been watching these guys for a long time, so we must be careful not to get in their way. But in the meantime, we still must prepare for the fight and make sure we are ready to go just in case."

Tyler nodded his approval.

"I think we need to make another visit tomorrow," Derek said. "Just to keep the pressure on. But we need to check with Terry first. Since they seem to be clueless as to how much we know, I believe they will continue to make their moves."

"Okay, Doc. I trust your judgment."

"And I trust Terry. He has a lot of connections. He knows a lot of people and he is respected in the community. We need to maintain our levelheadedness." Slowly rising from his chair, he covered a yawn and laid a hand on Tyler's shoulder. "Listen, get some rest. It's been a long day. I'm exhausted and I'm sure you are too."

Derek had only been asleep for a short time when the nightmare began. He desperately tried to open the heavy glass doors that were his

shield from what he saw taking place outside. Instinct told him that beyond this doorway lay another chapter of his life. Through the barrier, he beheld a procession of demonic creatures moving in a repeated circle—bouncing, hopping, and waving their arms. As one, they paused, bowed down and lifted the still body of the elderly shaman woman, as if offering her to unseen spirits. The ceremony continued until Spider stepped into the circle, holding aloft an angel figurine as he stared at the departed woman's remains.

Derek watched in fascination and horror, unable to tear his eyes away from the scene unfolding before him. He could hear drums and chanting, and he knew that this was a ceremony, a ritual of some kind. But he did not understand its purpose or meaning.

As the ceremony continued, Spider held aloft the angel figurine, its wings spread wide, as he stared at the departed woman's remains. His face was grave and solemn, and Derek could sense the weight of his grief.

Filled with a strange mixture of fear and fascination, Derek's gaze fixed on the inert body of the shaman woman. He felt a sense of reverence and respect for her, for the power she held, even in death. And in that moment, he knew that he had stumbled upon something sacred and mysterious, but then it hit him that he would never know how to get rid of his tattoos.

Derek came abruptly awake, coated in icy sweat. His heart pounded wildly against his ribs. He was still in his penthouse bedroom, albeit disoriented.

The quiet of the morning wasn't enough to calm his nerves as he lay still beneath his sheets. He felt another cold sensation, and the faint scent of herbs emanated into his room. Despite the familiarity of his surroundings, Derek knew something was off. Was he still in his dream or awake in his own bed? Anticipation coursed through him as he recalled the dream. He remembered standing at the entrance of his old school, watching a crowd of dark figures approach menacingly. Even after waking up, the lingering sense of dread made the small hairs on his arms and the back of his neck stand on end.

Finally mustering the courage to get out of bed, Derek slowly walked toward the window. He cautiously peered out, expecting to find the horde of shadows outside waiting for him. But the streets were empty. The dream was just a dream, and he was safe.

Taking a deep breath, he turned away from the window and put on a T-shirt. Even though his nightmare was over, its chill lingered in the air. He knew that he had to take action, learn what the dreams meant and why he was having them. He had a feeling the answer lay with the old shaman. He had to find out what was waiting for him—before she was no longer alive to help him.

On edge and unable to relax, he dressed and went down for his daily workout. As he ran on the treadmill, his mind kept going back to the demons in his dream. He sensed that they were knocking at the door of his soul. They haunted him relentlessly, but why?

He went through his customary shower ritual, scrubbing away any lingering insecurities from the day before. Once the stress of the previous day was gone, he stepped out and patted himself dry. The reason behind his increasing unease lay in all the unanswered connections. Like a spider web, one thread seemed to lead to another. He had to get to the center of it. He knew that he had to uncover the mystery that waited for him there. He would have to lean into whatever it was.

He emerged from his room a little more rejuvenated than when he had retired the night before. He wandered into the empty kitchen and poured himself a steaming cup of coffee.

When he opened the patio door and stepped outside, he was surprised to find Tyler had left for the day. The warm sun beamed down. A pleasant ocean breeze drifted across his skin. On days like this, Derek would usually find himself sitting out on the back porch of Kendal's place. It was one of those perfect mornings that he used to enjoy.

He stood on the balcony, with the cool tiles beneath his bare feet, and took in the cityscape with the ocean beyond. He stood there, bathed in warm sunlight and caressed by the gentle ocean breeze.

Inhaling deeply, Derek closed his eyes and let the salty air fill his lungs. He tried to push the memories away, to focus on the present moment. But somehow, the past always seemed to creep back in.

Suddenly, a stray thought crossed his mind—a fragment of a memory that he had long forgotten. A memory of his grandmother, standing on her patio, her hand reaching out to touch him . . . and then the memory faded, like a ghost disappearing into the mist.

Shaking his head, Derek opened his eyes and stepped back inside. He would have to let go of the past and the heartache it brought. But this morning somehow felt different—as if some small positive emotional memory from his past was trying to stir back to life. He felt invigorated by his workout with a new energy he hadn't experienced in quite some time.

He stood against the kitchen counter, running his fingers along the edges of his phone. It was time to call Kendal.

The call went to voicemail. He was a bit disappointed, but he left a message. He then poured his second cup of coffee. As he sat down at the center island bar, his cellphone rang—it was Father Mike.

"Top of the morning to you, Padre! How are you doing this beautiful morning?" Derek said in a cheerful voice.

"Doing well. You sound good. I became worried after you left so abruptly last night."

The reminder of the previous evening's events took a small bite of wind out of his sails. "She's definitely getting into my head, Father."

"What do you mean?"

"When I was sitting in the chair last night beside her bed, I dozed, I think. She came to me and said that I've left myself open to all of this."

"Did she seem to be intending you harm?" Father Mike asked.

"No, not exactly. I did get the impression that if I don't take care of something for her that there may be some sort of consequence, but she didn't really get that far."

"What exactly did she say?"

"She said she wants me to bring her granddaughter to her."

"Did she tell you where you can locate her granddaughter or who her granddaughter is?"

"No, I think that's the problem. I think she wants me to find her."

"Be careful." Father Mike's voice lowered. "This may come at a very high price. You could be dealing with a dark entity here. These demons are oriented to fulfilling their own selfish desires. Remember when you are in search of truth, you will inevitably come across God, who can bring immense fulfillment, peace, and joy into your life.

"Mark 11:24 says: *Therefore I tell you, whatever you ask for in prayer, believe that you have received it, and it will be yours.* What concerns me the most, Derek, is your underlying motivation. It's important to know exactly what you want in life and ask God to fulfill those desires. You should directly ask God for what you want. It should be in the context of a personal relationship with God rather than a vague 'Universe' force.

"When you make your requests, you must have faith that He hears you and will answer your prayers in His own way. You must also be cautious not to become too fixated on this thing you are asking for, as this can easily lead to idolatry. Hebrews 11:1 tells us, *Now faith is being sure of what we hope for and certain of what we do not see.* Always remember that God is the ultimate giver and source of all good gifts."

Derek's shoulders slumped. "But what other options do I have? It appears that she holds the key to how I can reclaim my life."

"She is separate from Divine Love," Father Mike assured him. "Her essence is darkness. Our Lord and Savior already paid the price for you. He is the key to getting your life back, just put your faith in Him."

Derek got up from his barstool at the counter and started to pace. "With all due respect Padre, I don't think this is His battle. She came after me and has a part of me that I need to get back from her. If she doesn't believe in my God, how will that help? I think I'm better off going after this one on my own."

"You have it backward. It's the opposite, she has attached herself to you." Father Mike corrected. "She hasn't taken anything from you."

Derek stopped pacing. "How can that be?"

"She is a part of an invisible energy that has attached itself to you through mutual attraction. She can provoke corresponding events around you by using invisible influence through dark energy."

Derek looked out at the horizon, the blue waters of the Pacific just visible in the distance. "Invisible influence through dark energy?"

"They are malevolent energies. They cause wars, diseases and suffering of all kinds. We know them to be the Beings of Darkness. They can hook to your energy, affecting your behavior. In your case it is happening because your personality has remained stuck in a specific place and period of time."

Derek automatically flashed back to the sidewalk where he was almost beaten to death. "A place and period of time," he repeated.

Father Mike continued, "This is the lost piece of your soul she is talking about. It's still in your being, but a part of your energy is detached and fixed to a distant location connected to your childhood. This was caused by your childhood trauma. Some amount of your subconscious attention has remained intensely preoccupied with the traumatic event and that site. It is important for you to let go of the pain and trauma to retrieve that lost part."

Derek threw his head back, exasperated. "How do I do that? This is starting to sound a lot like what Dr. Cole has been talking about."

Father Mike tried to explain in a way that Derek could understand. "This is achieved through a process that we call soul retrieval. Remember, we are always in charge of our own lives. Let me remind you that when you accepted Jesus into your heart, there was no adverse reaction from your soul. Jesus taught about the awareness of evil. He said the enemies need to be known.

"In the Bible, He spoke of a man out of whom a spirit came. The departed spirit was replaced by seven others even more wicked than itself. He compared that to a house that had been left empty only to be inhabited by far worse inhabitants. This means that right now you have Jesus in your heart and soul. If you kick Him out to handle this yourself and not rely on Him, then you have made room for not only her to enter but for more like her to join.

"In your case, I believe that all these events are related to your trauma. You need to be able to understand the nature of its attachment. One thing you must hang on to at all costs, *you are never alone*. You always have the Lord with you. You can call upon him at any time. He is the Father Almighty, maker of heaven and earth."

Derek absorbed all this for a moment. Then he sighed. "It does give me comfort to know that I have Him to fall back on. Because I have a feeling if this doesn't go right, I am going to need Him. How is the old woman doing today?"

"No change."

"That's disheartening. Okay, well thank you, Padre, for your support and guidance. I'll wait to hear from you."

Derek disconnected the call, and then looked up to see Tyler standing in the doorway. "Hey, good morning, where have you been?"

Tyler wiped his face with a small towel. "Working out, making sure I'm ready. I just took a break to get something to eat and then I'm going back."

"I could really use another workout. I was thinking I could be your sparring partner today."

Tyler retracted his head out of the refrigerator to answer. "That would be great."

"Thank God I went grocery shopping," Derek chuckled.

Chapter 12

Kendal sighed, taking in a deep breath of crisp morning air as she gathered her thoughts. On the deck chair, she hugged her knees while watching the sunrise.

It had been a difficult week, her first week alone after asking Derek to leave the apartment. She struggled to settle into the new routine of running the clinic by herself, while also devoting time to helping Derek figure out what was causing the strange changes to his body.

The tattoos that covered his skin were becoming increasingly hard to ignore, a constant reminder of the tragedy that had shadowed his life. Despite this, she remained steadfast in her commitment to help him find answers, determined to bring Derek back to some semblance of normalcy.

But when she sat at her desk, surrounded by stacks of paperwork and patients' charts, she couldn't help but feel a sense of hopelessness creeping in. The weight of Derek's situation and the burden of trying to solve it felt heavier with each passing day.

She closed her eyes, trying to find some sense of peace amidst the chaos. She knew she couldn't give up, even if the task seemed impossible. Derek needed her, and she couldn't let him down. Not when he was counting on her the most.

Yet it was becoming increasingly difficult to keep her emotional distance, to remain just friends. She yearned to be able to do more but held herself back, knowing how vulnerable he was feeling.

Kendal vacillated on whether the relationship was worth salvaging. She wanted to put up a good fight to make it work, but she wasn't sure she could take it much longer because it felt like her efforts were being thwarted. Sometimes she was tempted to throw in the towel. Yet ... she did want to see it through—no matter what happened.

Just like in kickboxing matches, even though she might not emerge the victor, she knew she had done everything she could to stay in the fight.

"Sometimes we need to stand our ground and defend our own mental wellbeing. And if things don't go our way, at least we gain wisdom and experience," she told herself as she rose slowly from her chair to get ready for work.

Kendal stepped out of the surgical room and quietly closed the door behind her. She had been assisting Dr. Lee with a nose reconstruction procedure. She took her gloves off and slowly washed her hands in the sink, letting the warm water run over her hands and arms as she thought about the last few days.

Kendal had been wearing a lot of hats lately. Not only was she trying to be there for the doctors and nurses in the clinic, but she was also trying to be there for Derek. He had been struggling, though he was doing his best to stay positive. The truth was, she was exhausted.

As the water cascaded down the drain, Kendal took a deep breath, willing her mind to find the strength to get through the rest of the day. She ran her hands over her face, feeling the familiar creases of fatigue, then turned off the faucet and headed back out into the hallway to go to the supply room to start inventory.

The sun was slowly setting when she stepped into her small apartment with an armload of paperwork from the office. She dropped the stack of papers on the entrance table, turned on the light, and flipped the switch for the ceiling fan. She opened the sliding glass door and the room filled with a cool ocean breeze.

Brutus, her white cockatoo, squawked from his perch in the cage. She reached in and grabbed his water bowl. She went to the sink and rinsed it out then filled it with fresh water. She did the same with his seed.

The pleasurable smell of the salt air started to relax her immediately. She had been running from one task to the next since early morning. Her mind was still filled with a jumble of figures, calculations, and problem-solving that had left her buzzing.

But despite the hectic day, her thoughts now turned elsewhere—to Derek. She opened the refrigerator and took out leftover Chinese from the night before. She left the food in the containers and placed them all in the microwave. She stood in deep thought as the boxes went around on the turntable in the small window.

It had been a few weeks since she had first stepped in and offered to help, and the situation was becoming much more complicated than she had anticipated. Her time and energy were now spent entirely on running the clinic and supporting Derek; she was starting to feel the strain of the load.

Kendal had stepped into the relationship with her eyes wide open, or so she thought. But as time passed and her feelings for him grew ever stronger, she could not help but start to doubt herself. She had been hurt before, and yet here she was, allowing herself to be vulnerable again.

Every time he gazed into her green eyes with his own baby blues, her doubts melted away. She felt her heart swell with joy every time he touched her gently, brushed a lock of her hair away from her face, or merely locked eyes with her in a way that seemed to be saying, "We can take on the world, together."

The microwave pinged and came to a stop. She reached in to grab the boxes and burnt one of her fingers. She rushed over to the sink to run some cold water over it. She stood looking out to the deck as the cool water soothed the burn.

She couldn't help but feel a sense of apprehension mixed with disappointment after their last argument. Even though he seemed to genuinely care for her, she questioned if she'd gotten too involved too quickly. She thought that maybe if she'd taken a step back and gone slower, she wouldn't find herself alone in this awkward situation. But it was probably too late. All she could do now was observe the progression of events.

She turned off the water and dried her hands on a dish towel. She took the boxes out of the microwave and set them on the counter. She opened each box carefully, letting the steam rise out, and grabbed a fork, electing to eat directly from the boxes.

She had made a habit of protecting herself from the pain and disappointment that came with failed relationships, carefully cultivating an emotional distance that allowed her to face the world without too much vulnerability. But now, with Derek so close to her heart, she realized how easily she could get hurt.

Not paying attention to what she was putting in her mouth, she had to spit out a chili pepper into the sink. She picked up the box of white rice and took a bite to dissipate the burn of the pepper in her mouth. She took a long drink of water and continued to eat.

Kendal was drawn to the intensity of his emotions like a moth to a flame, but she also knew deep down that it wasn't going to end well. When he had become more unstable, she decided to make sure she was always prepared to walk away. She had to remember to watch out for herself, too. The emotional investment she was making in the relationship might not work out. She needed to be emotionally equipped for whatever the outcome would be.

She threw the empty boxes into the trash. Wiped down the counter and washed her fork. She picked up her glass of water and took one last sip, dumped the rest then set her glass in the sink.

But even as she had these thoughts, she couldn't bring herself to take a step away from him. His hands were strangely comforting when they held hers and his voice soothed her doubts when he whispered to her in the dark. She was drawn to him, to his passion and energy, and she was afraid that once she moved away, she wouldn't be able to find her way back.

She picked up the stack of papers and folders and set them down on the breakfast counter. Then she went to her bedroom to change her clothes. She threw the day's scrubs into the hamper and stepped into the shower.

A fondness and admiration had quickly developed into a deep bond between them. But she had to remember that it could just as quickly disappear. No matter how strong her feelings for him were, she had to make sure she was the one in control of her own emotions.

She wanted desperately to continue to help Derek unravel his tangled web of issues, but at the same time was hesitant to get too close to him in the process. Though the two of them had grown close over the past month, it had become obvious to her that the relationship was still too fresh for either of them to consider anything other than friendship.

Kendal pulled on her favorite sweats. Relaxed, full, and comfortable, she padded back out to attack the stack of papers awaiting her.

Still, she couldn't help but wonder what might happen if the two of them allowed themselves to lean into one another, trusting in the connection they had forged. She was afraid that in doing so, they might be risking more than either one was willing to admit.

There was still a long way to go before she could feel that he was ready for a long-term personal relationship. She didn't want to put herself in a situation that she might not be able to get out of without severe damage to her growth and development. She debated the pros and cons of continuing to date Derek, knowing that if she did, she would have to take the relationship slowly and carefully so as not to rush into something that she wasn't yet ready for.

She picked up the first folder and tried to focus on the patient's information, but her mind wasn't ready to go there yet. Instead, she elected to break up the pile into stacks of priority.

Although she could feel the connection between them deepening, she was also watching to see signs of growth and improvement in his thought process. He needed to be much more open with talking about his feelings, and he needed to understand the importance of communication in a relationship. The relationship between them had always been complicated. Being business associates certainly had its benefits, but it was also trying.

They had built a reliable business rapport. Yet, on the other hand, the balancing act of being a business associate as well as his girlfriend was proving to be quite difficult. The lines were blurred.

Every interaction was a battle to remain professional. She was constantly aware of the need to be careful with her words and actions. He was similarly cautious, likely due to the same battle. Every conversation seemed laced with potential landmines. She could feel his frustration with her as well. He was becoming more guarded around her. This wasn't necessarily a bad thing. It prevented him from having the green light to just take his emotions and throw up all over her anytime he felt the urge.

Nevertheless, they had both managed to remain on an even footing. They kept their conversations civil, and sometimes even productive. But the emotional bedlam was always there, simmering beneath the surface, ready to boil over at any moment.

Once the folders and papers were stacked into their individual piles, Kendal realized she needed her pen. She found her little backpack purse sitting in the corner of the chair where she had tossed it when she walked in. She unzipped the topmost zipper and rummaged around for her favorite pen. Then she fished her cellphone from the outer pocket and checked for any messages she might have received while she was in the shower.

Though she had started to feel like they could have a future together, she knew that she needed more time to evaluate before making up her mind. Since he had moved out of her small apartment, she had started to go on evening runs, letting her thoughts wander and carefully examining her feelings for Derek. Tonight, she would focus on paperwork instead.

In the end, her resolution had been as clear as the night sky above her. She knew that she wanted to continue to have him in her life—issues and all—and to see where their relationship could take them.

Despite everything they had been through, she knew that their friendship would persevere. Regardless of how perplexing it became or how much strain was placed upon it, she still held onto the idea that they would be friends. Their bond would remain constant, and she would always be there for him.

Tonight, rather than continuing to dwell on their relationship or lack thereof, Kendal needed to focus. She put the cellphone on the counter.

Derek was depending on her, and she could not let him down. With a renewed sense of purpose, she set about going through the patients' files she would need for the next day. She worked with a focused intensity, clearing her mind of everything but the tasks at hand.

When the sun had completely disappeared and the night sky had settled, Kendal looked at the stack of papers and folders on the counter and felt a sense of satisfaction. She had been able to organize and prepare the patient files and she was ready to tackle whatever the next day would bring.

With one last deep sigh, Kendal left the finished stack on the breakfast bar. Turned off the lights in the living room and headed to the bathroom to prepare for bed. When she finally settled under her blanket, she immediately drifted off into a much-needed deep sleep.

Chapter 13

At the gym, Derek and Tyler went straight to the mat to warm up. It had been a while since Derek had taken the opportunity to spar with anyone. He could feel the tremendous power in each of Tyler's blows. It was humbling—but exactly what Derek needed. It reinforced in him the power of the human spirit.

Tyler continued to drill and work his way around the gym as Derek did his best to assist. After a couple of hours, they stopped to rest and hydrate.

"I want to go with you when you go back over to the house to meet these guys." Tyler wiped the sweat from his face, then took another drink from his water bottle.

"I don't think that's such a good idea," Derek replied.

"He's my brother. I need to make sure he's all right." Tyler gave a hard elbow punch to the bag.

Derek held the heavy punching bag in position. "Yeah, but they like to antagonize you, which could jeopardize the deal."

Tyler spun and hit the bag with the back of his heel. "How do you know that they are doing something that their bosses don't know about?"

Derek absorbed the blow, pushing him back with the power of the kick. "I don't. We must go by what our sources are telling us."

"When I lived in Thailand, I would go to the Muay Thai boxing gym every day. My trainer had me enter the ring to challenge myself against someone who would want to knock my block off." With a backfist punch, he continued, "I followed my training and preparation like a ritual. I had good days and bad days. I stuck with it and worked until I was ready for my first organized match, having, of course, done plenty of sparring in advance."

He gave a leaping kick, knocking Derek and the bag forcefully back. "In my Muay Thai matches, I had to overcome my anxiety and fear of facing the unknown. In my imagination, I would see my competitor as a beast of a fighter who might break my nose or knock me out. There was the potential for him to embarrass me in front of my own family. But in spite of all that, I still entered the ring."

He grabbed the bag with both hands and gave it a Muay Thai knee bomb. "When I started to fight, the nerves fell away. Once that bell sounded the only thing I could see was standing immediately in front of me. My focus was a laser on the action that unfolded in split-second timing. It was a total rush. I would always hope that it would lead me to victory, and it did. But then I found out that I wanted more from my life!"

Derek let the bag go. "They wouldn't have asked for this second meeting if they weren't trying to find out how much we really know."

"Well, I don't want to push this too far. My only concern is to get my brother out of there alive."

"I understand." Derek picked up the boxing kick pads and prepared himself for the incoming blow. "Believe me, we all want the same thing."

Later that afternoon, when Derek returned home from the workout session, Terry picked him up in the old truck. They drove to the gang's hangout and pulled into the front yard, the crunching of gravel under the wheels stirring the zombie drug addicts who were lying around on old couches. Two men, clad in all black and wearing bandanas on their heads, stood guard at the entrance.

Terry turned off the engine and turned to Derek. "You ready for this?" he asked, his hand hovering over the door handle.

Derek didn't respond, but simply nodded, his jaw set in determination. Terry opened the truck door. The two men standing guard eyed them warily but made no move to stop them.

Derek and Terry stood in front of the two men. "Is your boss here?" Derek asked.

"Who wants to know?" the man asked, looking down from the porch.

"He should be expecting me. Tell him the Tatman is here."

Terry and Derek kept their eyes on the zombie people sprinkled around the yard. Both men knew that junkies were unpredictable; they could become violent and attack perfect strangers for no apparent reason.

The man opened the door. "He'll see you." He held the door open as Terry and Derek cautiously stepped inside the house, the man then closed and locked the door behind them. As they entered, the pungent smell of drugs hit them like a physical force.

It was deathly still inside but for the ticking of an old decrepit grandfather clock in the corner. A sudden movement drew their attention to a dark corner, where a young man with a scraggly beard stood with a blank expression on his face watching them.

The walls were lined with peeling wallpaper. Yet, despite the squalor, there was an air of danger and power permeating the place. Derek and Terry were led through the maze of rooms until they reached their destination.

The man motioned for them to enter. The room was lit with a soft, yellow light from flames in the fireplace on the far wall. In the center stood a large mahogany desk, and behind it stood the same pale-faced Asian man, but this time in a simple black suit and wearing a stern expression. A psychological game seemed to be in play. He stared across the room at them, his gaze never wavering, and nodded for them to sit in the two wooden chairs in front of the desk.

Terry and Derek glanced at each other. This wasn't what they had expected to find when coming to this house. They both felt a growing sense of apprehension as the man behind the desk slowly walked around to the front, stopping a few steps away from them.

He cleared his throat and spoke in a quiet yet firm voice. "Tatman, I understand you have something to show me? Have a seat."

He appeared to treat their arrival as a special ceremonial occasion—a shift from their last meeting. Derek took a seat directly in front of the man. Terry elected to stand.

"How's our Magic Monk doing?" he asked. "Is he ready to fight?"

Derek nodded solemnly, playing along. "Yes, he's ready."

"Good. We don't want any misunderstandings." He acted as though he held an unspoken power and that he sat in the seat of judgment. "He needs to bring his best tomorrow. The magic needs to be in full force or else there are going to be some serious repercussions."

Derek was unfazed by this show of intimidation. "You need to understand that if all of this doesn't go down the way it is supposed to, then *you* are going to have to answer some questions," he countered.

His smile disappeared. "What questions would those be?"

"Now *that,* I wouldn't know, I can only provide the facts and then let your bosses ask the questions."

"And what facts would those be?" He frowned, lips tightening.

"Well, for now those facts are put away in a safe place, so that if anything happens to Magic Monk or his brother, or anyone associated with them, the facts go directly to your bosses." Derek stared back at him with a half-smile. "I have it set up on a failsafe system. If anything should happen, I won't even be able to stop it. So, let's not push that button."

"Why should I believe you?" He crossed his arms as he leaned back.

"I am here on mutual trust." Derek maintained eye contact. "I trust that you are going to do what you say you will do, and you trust that I will do what I say I will do. That's all."

Speaking slowly in a controlled voice, he asked, "How do I know when this is over, you won't use that information?"

Derek stiffened. "The same way I know that when this is all over, you are not going to come after us for more money."

He forced a smile. "Okay, I get it. *Trust.* So, we are going to make this one deal and then it's over."

Derek returned the smile. "That's the idea, yes."

He nodded and returned to his place behind the desk. "Okay, be at The Lodge in Studio City, 8 p.m. sharp tomorrow night. Meet at the side entrance. My guys will be there to take him in to get him ready. I don't want anyone with him before the fight except one of my guys." He pointed his finger at Derek. "You got it?"

"No." Derek sat relaxed. "I stay with him at all times. I am his coach and sparring partner. What happens after the fight?"

The man inhaled a controlled breath and slowly blinked, then sat down in his chair. "Okay, Tatman, but just you. Once we collect our money, then he will be free to go."

"What about his brother?" Derek asked, glancing back at Terry.

"He still owes me money," the man said.

"I want this all to end tomorrow night. Plan to release him at the same time." Derek resisted the impulse to clench his fists.

"Okay, all the better." He smirked as if he knew something Derek had missed.

"You just make sure that the kid is in good condition and that they both come back healthy." Derek rose to leave, then turned back. "What do I call you? What's your name?"

"My name is ZhiZhu. You know, like the Spiderman." He made a climbing motion with his hands.

"Spiderman?" Derek's eyes went wide. He tried to control his emotional reaction to the name.

"Yeah, like the guy who climbs the buildings. His name is ZhiZhu, they call him Spiderman."

"Okay, ZhiZhu, Spiderman, let's get this done."

As they exited the front door, he heard the lock snap closed behind them. Derek's senses felt weirdly heightened. He noticed a girl with a large birthmark on her face standing at the corner of the house.

"Wait here a minute," he told Terry.

Terry stopped. His head swiveled to survey their surroundings as Derek walked to the corner of the house.

Derek approached her slowly. "Hi there, I am Dr. Hollinger. You know, I can remove that for you." He tilted his head to examine the birthmark.

"You can? But you don't look like a doctor." She put her hand up to her face, looking around to make sure no one was watching.

"It might take a couple of procedures, but I can take care of it for you." He smiled. "And I assure you, I am an excellent plastic surgeon."

"I'm cursed. Won't it just come right back?" Tears welled in her eyes.

"I have removed many of them and not one has ever come back."

"But they told me that this is because of the sins of my family. I am cursed because of the past," she said, looking down at her hands.

He shook his head. "This is not from sin." Derek held a palm up as if to take her hand. "It is simply a birthmark that can be removed."

She shrunk back. "I have no way to pay you," she said with a quaver in her voice. At that moment her gaze shifted, and Derek could see the panic in her eyes. They were being watched.

He quickly reached into his pocket. "Take my card," he said, slipping it to her discreetly. In a low voice, he urged, "Call me. Don't worry about money." Then he turned and walked back to Terry. "Let's get out of here."

Terry glanced back; she was already gone.

At the penthouse, Derek immediately placed a call to Kendal.

She picked up on the first ring. "Hey, how are you?" she asked cheerfully. "I was just about to call you back. You must have E.S.P."

"How are you doing?" He wished he could reach out and touch her. Derek heard her take a deep breath.

"Staying crazy busy."

"Lots to report. Can I see you tonight?" His heart began to race.

"Sure, I'm almost done," she said in a matter-of-fact voice.

"Would you like to join me for a drink?" He could hear his voice raise in pitch, and he shut his eyes, cringing inwardly at the implications of his suggestion.

She hesitated. "Should I come over to you or do you want to come over to my place?"

"I'm still not ready to go back to your place and since I don't know what Tyler has planned, let's just meet for a drink."

It felt awkward to say it. He hoped she wouldn't think he was being rude. Setting boundaries felt uncomfortable. But after their last encounter at the penthouse, he didn't want to put himself in a position that would end in another turn-down.

"How about that little restaurant with the outside patio, down on the beach? In about a half hour?" she suggested.

"Great, I'll see you there."

Chapter 14

When Derek arrived at the restaurant, Kendal was seated at a table close to the sand. She smiled and waved. He felt butterflies in his stomach as he approached and bent to kiss her.

"Hello, handsome," she said, putting her hand on the top of her fedora and kissing him on the cheek.

"You sure are in a good mood today." He felt his body relax.

"I am. The office is running smoothly, and now that I am out here on the beach having a drink, I'm a happy camper." She smiled and took a sip of her fruit-laced sangria.

"Okay, I want whatever you're having." He smiled.

After the waiter took his order, Derek leaned back in the chair and took a deep breath. Kendal watched him as she took another sip from her fruit-lined glass. He tilted his head back and put his sunglasses up onto his cap to soak in the sun on his face. The waiter came back to drop off his glass of sangria.

"Cheers, to a beautiful day at the beach," Kendal said as Derek picked up his glass.

"Cheers." Derek clicked his glass against hers and took a sip. "Um, that's good."

She turned her seat toward him. "So, what's going on?" She looked into his eyes, searching for some indication of his mental status.

"So much, you just wouldn't believe." He could feel her probing for something deeper than he was able to give in that moment. He looked down at his glass, trying to decide where to begin.

"Well, start with the old lady. Have you been to the hospital lately to see her?" Kendal was tired, it had been a long day, and she didn't have the patience to pussyfoot around.

"Yeah, I went again last night. It got pretty crazy. Father Mike was there. We decided we would take turns staying by her bed. I took the first shift. I was kind of tired. I think I dozed off. I had a dream or a vision or something. She came to me and talked to me while I was asleep."

"Oh no, don't tell me that. I hate that kind of stuff." Kendal cringed, then took a big swig of her sangria.

"The old woman said that my soul had been compromised and that she found me because my childhood trauma had basically left me vulnerable when a piece of my soul fled—or something like that."

"That doesn't even make sense." She shook her head. "How can you even function without your soul?" She sat back in her chair. "And how would she be able to find you out of all the people in the world?" She took another sip. "You sure it was her talking to you and not your subconscious just messing with you?"

"Oh, yeah, it was her all right. There's more." Derek gulped his drink. "She said she wanted something from me."

"What? Hang on, something doesn't seem right." Kendal flagged the waiter for two more drinks as he passed their table. "She doesn't even know you. How can she ask you for something? What does she want?"

He leaned in with both arms on the table. "Her granddaughter," he said in a low voice.

Kendal leaned in closer. "Who is her granddaughter?"

Derek sat back. "I'm not sure." His shoulders slumped. "I haven't been able to figure that one out yet. And look at this." He reached into his front pants pocket and pulled out the little angel figurine, setting it on the table.

"That's cute, where did you get it?" She picked it up.

"I made it." He grinned.

"Wow, that's pretty good." She turned it back and forth in her hand. "I didn't know you could whittle things out of wood." She set it back down.

The waiter set their drinks in front of them and walked away.

"I can't whittle anything." Derek grabbed his cap, lifted it and sat it back on his head, setting his sunglasses on the table. "I mean I could when I was a kid." He picked up the angel figurine. "I made this right before I was attacked. I was carrying it in my backpack as a gift for my grandmother." He inspected it more closely. "I had forgotten all about it until I found it sitting on the nightstand of the old lady." He set it back down in the middle of the table.

"That's unbelievable." Kendal picked it up. "How could that be?"

"Well, it's a long story, but Spider had it. He's been carrying it around for all these years."

Her eyes went wide. "Shut up."

"Yeah." He pulled at the bottom of his ear. "I guess he used it as a good luck charm or something."

"This just keeps getting weirder." Kendal looked at the angel in her hand. "What do you think *his* connection is to the old lady?"

"I'm not sure." Derek's jaw clenched. "But I'm going to find out."

"What did she say about her granddaughter?" Kendal set the

angel figurine down, searching his face for any hint of anxiety.

"Nothing really. Just that if I want my soul, that I had better get her granddaughter back to her."

"Does she think you took her, or something?"

Derek swallowed a groan. "No, I don't think so. I didn't get that impression."

"Did she put the tattoos on you?"

"She seemed to indicate that they are a result of something else. When she spotted me in front of the hotel, she said she was attempting to reconnect with the piece of my soul that had gone missing, supposedly to help it return to me." He let his head fall sideways, shaking it slightly. "When I severed ties with her, all my emotions and experiences scattered, or something. They had no way to reconnect, so they're now displayed across my skin."

"That sounds far-fetched," Kendal replied, crossing her arms. "So, if you bring her granddaughter back to her, then you get your soul back? And your emotions and experiences will have a place to go and your skin will go back to normal. Am I hearing this correctly?"

"That's what she made it sound like—I'm not sure." His cellphone rang. He looked at the caller ID. "Sorry, I'd better take this. Hello?"

"Hello, Dr. Hollinger? This is Ami Soo."

"Ami Soo?" He raised a quizzical brow at Kendal.

"Yes, with the birthmark?"

"Oh, yes, Ami Soo! How are you?" He stood and made a one-minute motion to Kendal as he walked away. "I am so happy to hear from you. When can you come in for a consultation to remove that birthmark?"

"Your office is downtown. I think I can get a ride."

"Can you come in tomorrow? The address is on my business card."

"Yes, I know, I think so."

"How about midmorning, 10 a.m.?" He looked over at Kendal, who sat at the table, staring out at the ocean.

In a soft tone, she said, "I will do my best."

"Wonderful, you will be happy you did."

"Please do not say anything to my brother," she pleaded in a hushed voice.

"Who is your brother?"

"ZhiZhu."

"Oh." The name caught him by surprise.

"I understand if you do not want to do it."

He hesitated, feeling trepidation. "No, no. I'll take care of you. Just try to be on time." Derek hung up and returned to the table.

"What was that all about?" Kendal's eyes filled with curiosity.

"I have a patient coming in tomorrow. Pro bono."

"Oh. Well, that's nice." She watched him as he began to bounce one leg nervously, waiting for the rest of the explanation.

"She has a birthmark on her face. She's only about eighteen years old and shouldn't have to live that way. But I just found out her brother is the head of the gang we are trying to get Tyler's brother away from." He laced his hands behind his neck.

"Uh-oh, do you think that is such a good idea?" Kendal put her hand to her mouth. "He might get upset?"

"Yeah, I just thought about that. But I promised her when I met her standing outside the house. I thought she was just one of the druggies hanging out. I was thinking that removing it might give her a chance at life." He rolled his head around to stretch his neck out. "Boy, what a fine mess I've got myself into."

"Well, now that you found out that she's *not* just one of the druggies and she is actually *the gang leader's sister*, I suggest you call it off before someone gets hurt or worse." Kendal pursed her lips and crossed her arms.

"No." He shook his head. "I won't to do that. It's not her fault that she has a criminal for a brother."

"When is she coming in?"

"Tomorrow," he said flatly.

She leaned forward. "I'm going to be there with you."

"No." He shook his head slowly. "I don't think that is a good idea."

"Well, I do," Kendal replied stubbornly. "That way the brother can't accuse you of something other than trying to help his sister, if I'm there."

He cocked his head. "You might have a point." Derek took a swallow of his drink. "Tomorrow is only a consultation. With the clinic closed on weekends I thought it would be the perfect time to do some pro bono work without any questions."

"That's even better. Then we can establish a relationship and try to figure out how all of this is going to work with her brother in the picture." Kendal had finished her drink and picked at the fruit at the bottom of the glass. "Where are her parents?"

"Not a clue. Those are some of the questions I can ask her tomorrow." He smiled. "Thank you. I appreciate your help."

"I told you I would be here for you." Her smile faded. "Just don't try to shut me out when it comes to the business."

They sat at the table for a minute looking out at the ocean.

Derek was first to speak. "I am still confused as to where we stand."

Kendal took a deep breath. "All I am saying is for right now, don't worry about me. I am here for you. Let's see if we can get some of this sorted out and there will be time for us later."

"I hope so." He looked at her longingly.

"If it is meant to be, then it will be. Only God knows what the future holds." She brushed back a strand of hair from her face.

"That's what Father Mike has been telling me."

"Are you talking to Father Mike now?"

"He's been counseling me through all of this. It helps to have a spiritual opinion on the matter. He and Dr. Cole are on the same page with the information they are giving me."

Kendal fiddled with the strands of auburn hair peeking out from beneath her hat. "I'm just starting to take some time to figure out where I stand with my relationship with God. I think that's what's missing in my life. So, I have gone back to church, and it feels good."

"Good for you. I'm still in the first phase of trying to figure out my relationship with God."

She locked eyes with him. "Let me know if you would like to go sometime. It is a great church, great music, and you can really feel the Shekinah when you walk in the door."

He sat there looking deep into her eyes but didn't say anything.

She glanced down at her hands. "So, what is your next step with the old woman?"

"I get the feeling I am being led down a dark road." He stared intently out at the ocean. "It seems I'm being left breadcrumbs to let me know that I am on the right path."

Kendal looked up and studied him. "What do you mean?"

"Well, the night of the plastic surgeon awards, I encountered the kids in the crosswalk, who provoked me by attempting a carjack. This sent me into an anxiety attack related to my childhood trauma. I then had a scuffle with the old woman, who during this anxiety attack was trying to attach to my soul."

Derek suppressed a shudder. "I went through thirty-six hours of sheer hell. I woke up illustrated head to toe. I then connect with you, and we go down to San Diego where I run into Spider and Father Mike. Father Mike is taking care of both Spider and the old woman. Before Spider dies, he gives my angel to his roommate, who gives it to the old woman. Now, the old woman is about to die. All of this is because she says she is looking for her granddaughter. Right? But it started *before* I ran into the old woman. What am I missing here?" He rubbed his face in thought.

"Oh, and don't forget your premonition that almost got me killed the other day," Kendal added with a wince.

"You mean prevented you from being killed the other day." He shot her a side glance.

"Yes, of course."

"How is all of this linked?" He played idly with the cellphone in his hand. "How can I find the next breadcrumb?"

"I don't think you have to find it. They seemed to be dropped right in front of you."

"That's true. I guess I just need to keep my eyes open and stay aware."

"Yes, it seems that God is guiding you as you go."

"I just don't want to make a wrong move and end up going in the wrong direction."

"You shouldn't look at it that way. You just need to stay focused on the fact that these premonitions and experiences are coming to you and stay aware and deal with them as they come. Try not to let doubt and fear get in the way. You have been there before and it just messes with your head."

He sighed. "You're right, I just have to have faith that all of this is going to work out in the end."

Kendal nodded encouragingly. "Yes, that's right, look at what's happening. Look how you have the angel figurine back! That should give you the reassurance that everything is starting to work out."

"I hope so. I made it to give to my grandmother as a memorial gift for my father." He swallowed a lump. "But now she's gone."

"But what else could it be? I believe that God is giving you the assurance that he is working with you. He is helping you to overcome whatever it is that is working against you."

"That's what Father Mike is telling me." He balled up the cocktail napkin and threw it on the table in front of him.

"Then listen to Father Mike," Kendal urged gently. "I am sure he has a better handle on all of this than we do."

"That's why I was hoping to see you today. You give me the inspiration I need."

With a half-smile, she said, "That's what friends are for."

"Ouch, that hurts." He stood.

"What, now I'm not your friend?" She looked up at him, her hand shielding her eyes to block the sun.

"I've got to go." He grabbed his sunglasses off the table, trying to cover his hurt feelings. "See you at the office in the morning."

Kendal watched from her patio seat as Derek walked out to his bike in the parking lot. It took everything she had not to jump up and run after him.

Chapter 15

Ami Soo arrived at the clinic on time, with a young man in tow. He was dressed in a simple oversized white T-shirt and a baseball cap. The young man appeared to be somewhat out of his element, as if he were more accustomed to being in the shadows than in the spotlight.

Kendal recognized the sub-standard quality of the ink on his face as prison tattoos. She had done some internet research for Derek and learned that the tattooing equipment in prison had to be improvised. The ink was taken from wherever the inmates could steal it—pens, melted plastic, soot mixed with shampoo, even melted Styrofoam.

Glancing back at the pair following her to Derek's office, she recognized one of the many tattoos. The five dots on his neck confirmed he had done time in prison. They were known as a "quincunx." She had read that the four dots on the outside represent four walls, with the fifth on the inside representing the prisoner. With a queasiness that told her this decision to help Ami Soo was worse than she thought, she escorted them back to Derek's office.

"Good morning, Ami Soo, how are you this morning?" Derek stood up from behind his desk and motioned for the couple to come in.

Ami Soo fidgeted slightly with her hands, as if unsure of their decision. With an uneasy feeling, Kendal closed the door behind the young couple and stood back in the corner, her hands clasped trying not to be noticed.

Her escort turned his prison-tattooed face toward Kendal. His cold eyes stared back at her. She felt her stomach sink and tried to keep her expression calm.

He turned back to look at Derek. "I don't like her standing back there."

Kendal nonchalantly stepped forward to come around the desk to stand next to Derek. It was all she could do to keep her body relaxed.

"I'm Dr. Hollinger." He stretched out his tattooed hand across the desk.

With a tattooed-sleeved arm, the man reached out to clasp the doctor's hand. With a firm yank, he said, "What do you want with my girl?"

The handshake pulled Derek off balance. He put the other hand down on his desk for balance. With a blank expression, he replied, "I am going to remove the birthmark from her face." Derek knew this was a gesture of intimidation. He held his eyes and spread his fingers to signal he wanted to be released.

The man let go of his hand. "You don't look like a doctor to me."

"You're right." Derek kept a neutral expression. "I definitely don't look like a doctor. But I am, and this is my office."

"Why?" The man sat down. "What's she done for you?" He leered over at Ami Soo, who stood with her head hung low.

Derek sat down. In a firm voice, he said, "She has done nothing to deserve my attention. I like to help people occasionally. I thought that she might like to have this birthmark removed."

"She isn't no charity case. I take care of her." He gave her a sinister glance.

"I completely understand." Derek nodded in agreement. "But this is not charity. It's about Ami Soo having a better quality of life without having to live with the mark on her face."

"Is she going to have a scar?"

"No, she shouldn't. Sometimes there could be a little bit of discoloration but that's about it, no scars." He smiled gently looking in her direction. "It's a laser process. It will just take a couple of sessions."

The ex-con grabbed her face. "What if it comes back?"

"It will not come back." Derek looked Ami Soo in the eye and said in an overly exaggerated relaxed tone, "I have done quite a few of these and none of them have come back."

"I told you, Angel," Ami Soo said in a soft voice.

Angel relaxed. "Okay, what does she have to do?"

"We just need to give her an examination." Derek softened his gaze. "We need to take a closer look to see how deep the birthmark goes and how many sessions it is going to take to remove it."

Angel gave Ami Soo a calculating look. "Okay, but I'm staying with her."

Derek replied in an even tone, "No problem." He was trying to be very careful not to let Angel see that he was starting to get under his skin. He looked at Kendal and smiled. "Can you please take them to an examining room for me?"

Kendal kept her head high and back straight to give an outward appearance of calm professionalism. She opened the door to the hall and waited for the couple. She could feel her heart racing, her mouth dry. She wanted to help but also knew the consequences of going against the mafia. She wanted to trust these young people, but there was too much at stake. Still, she knew Derek couldn't bring himself to turn them away.

Kendal had stood back in the corner of the examination room, trying her best to blend in. She watched as Angel and Ami Soo exchanged words, his voice a low, menacing growl. A chill ran through her body. She had seen that look before.

It was the same look her mother's second husband used to give her when he was angry. He had been abusive and cruel, hitting her mother and intimidating Kendal. He had lived with them from when she was five to eight years old, and she remembered that shrinking feeling whenever he glared at her.

The memories of those days came flooding back in the face of Angel's menacing expression. She had thought she'd left that feeling of fear and dread behind her, yet here it was again, twisted and raw. Her throat constricted as she fought back tears. She felt a lump form in her chest as she trembled in the corner. She was rooted to the spot, unable to move until the examination was over.

The familiar sense of shame bubbled up inside. *Stop blaming yourself for the abuse*, she reminded herself. *Give your shame back to your abuser.*

Kendal had studied abuse in nursing school and how to recognize it. She had read that she needed to have self-compassion. In her later teen years, she was able to set limits.

The traumatic experiences continued with her mother's third husband, but she was older and able to thwart sexual targeting. Her symptoms of abuse had been managed and remained dormant until today. But her childhood trauma symptoms could still be triggered. She still suffered from the post-traumatic stress disorder that comes from being in a prolonged environment of abuse.

After the examination and consultation, the removal appointment was set. He determined that it would take three visits. The first would take place later that afternoon. Giving the couple a little time to discuss it, they left. Kendal walked back to Derek's office with trepidation, fearing what it would bring.

She pushed the feelings aside and focused on Derek. "Well, I hope this doesn't come back to bite you." Kendal sat down in the chair in front of his desk. "I can't help but have a bad feeling that this isn't going to end well."

"Ah, it will all be okay." He sat with hands behind his head, acting oblivious to Angel's abuse. "How can anyone be upset about making a young girl's life better?"

"Someone who controls her through her perceived disability. Maybe this has been her curse—causing her to be more dependent." Kendal understood emotional maltreatment. "She probably doesn't go too far from home because of the stigma, especially in her culture."

Derek's eyes twinkled. "Well, if you're right then I guess I'll have to deal with ZhiZhu when that time comes."

"Yeah, but you have other people to consider." She looked him in the eye and raised her eyebrows slightly. "What about Tyler and his brother?"

Derek looked away from Kendal, a hint of doubt in his voice. "I don't think this is going to affect them," he said, unsure of how far he should go with his pro bono work for Ami Soo.

But Ami Soo was relying on him—he could not ignore her implicit trust. He had vowed to help her. It seemed like a small thing and Derek was determined to stand by her and do what he could to relieve her of the burden of the birthmark on her face. He had felt her struggle, and he wanted to do something to help.

He looked at Kendal and forced a smile, pushing away his doubts. "It's worth a try," he said, his voice firmer now. He paused for a moment before continuing. "I will do whatever I can to help." Ami Soo had faith in him, and he had found strength in himself to give her back the gift of a normal life.

Kendal pursed her lips. "Well, if this little bombshell blows up before you get his brother out of there, who knows what could happen."

Ami Soo and Angel returned to the office later that afternoon as scheduled. Derek and Kendal welcomed them warmly and showed them into the exam room. The procedure was relatively simple and took a little over an hour.

Once the first procedure was complete, Derek handed them a printed sheet of instructions and told them to come back the following day for a follow-up appointment. He knew he should perform the removal as quickly as possible in case there might be interference coming from her brother, ZhiZhu. He was well aware of the dangers of delaying the procedure.

Ami Soo thanked Derek for his sensitivity and understanding. As they left the clinic, Derek and Kendal were left with a sense of relief—combined with weariness from the stress of the situation.

Chapter 16

Terry Ford had spent his entire adult life as a Marine, going from one military mission to the next. He'd traveled across the globe, accumulating a wealth of combat experience—and more than a few strategies for wartime situations. He'd been shot twice and seen more battles than most Marines ever would.

Returning home to the States was an unusual experience. In the military, there was a certain order to things. With each mission, Terry had a purpose and a plan. But at home, it felt like he was adrift in an uncertain sea. The unfamiliarity of civilian life was overwhelming and disorienting at first.

The years had been good to him. He had to admit that despite his dissatisfaction at being forced to retire from the military, he ultimately had been successful. Joining the corps had been the only way he had known how to make a living, and his regimented lifestyle kept him focused and on track.

He had worked his way up the ranks steadily over the years, never taking more than he could handle, but never settling for less than he could achieve. He had never married, but it wasn't for lack of trying. He had had his share of relationships, but none of them seemed to be worth the commitment to him.

But as the years passed, he had started to feel the toll that his military lifestyle had taken on his body. He tired more easily and felt the aches and pains that aging and being shot twice brought on. He had never thought about retirement until his commanding officer strongly suggested it was time. He wasn't happy, but he had to admit that it was indeed time.

He had been smart enough through the years and had invested. He had money coming in from his businesses, buildings, and other rental properties. It would be enough to maintain his lifestyle with little financial stress. But still, when he first got out of the military, there was an uncertainty in his mind. What would come next? He had no experience with anything outside the military and had no idea how he would spend his days. He felt a little bit of fear creep up as he thought about the unknown ahead.

His first night living in the city of Los Angeles, Terry had to ignore the sirens outside. It was like coming back to a war zone. He blocked out the sound so that it didn't bother him; the noise barely registered as he lounged in his armchair in front of the television. That lasted for about a week before he jumped into action to get into the rhythm of living a normal, everyday life.

It had been six years since he opened his tattoo business and three since he opened the bar. Things had gone better than expected. His days were full and the cash he'd earned from his tattoos and bar was letting him live comfortably. He'd even managed to invest in more rental properties.

But more than money, Terry was content with the knowledge that he'd achieved security. He had good and loyal friends around him. He was able to help people and give them jobs. His businesses gave him plenty to do, and with his pension coming in, Terry was living a life of contented ease. Who could complain?

This latest situation with the kid from Thailand had him feeling excited about a mission again. Even though he didn't like getting involved with anyone's personal life, that is where he drew the line. He had his friends in the police department, most of whom he had served with. They had all kept in touch. Once a Marine always a Marine. They were like family. So when it had come time to get some intel on this group that was terrorizing this kid and his brother, he knew he was in a good position to help.

One night, sitting in the bar, he had told Derek and Kendal about his two decades of experience as an enlisted Marine. "I can confidently say that the Corps is ungrateful and dismissive for any activity you do, excluding what the command or its officers are looking for at that very moment. You can work hard and with skill, trying to get the job done perfectly, but it won't mean anything unless it appeals to the Commander. The mission comes first and nothing else matters!" He chomped down hard on his unlit cigar.

Both Derek and Kendal seemed surprised at Terry's description of his service. But he continued to explain.

"You have to give your all and push yourself beyond the limits for many reasons like your own pride, feeling part of something bigger than just yourself, your squad or platoon mates, and the fact that if you don't perform at your best, it could cost you or someone who matters to you their life. In the Marine Corps, failure is not an option! There's an old saying in the Corps: 'Don't quit, never give up! Don't accept defeat—fight until the end.'" He took a hard swig of his beer.

They had been sitting at the bar for a while discussing how they had come to work in their chosen professions. After Derek and Kendal told their stories, they were surprised when Terry started to share.

"When I was in the Corps, I often worked for long stretches at a time—sometimes up to sixteen hours without eating and with few breaks. I had no idea why I was doing it beyond the assumed reason that it was needed for mission success. I also remember being in operations where I worked tirelessly for two days straight, seldom getting any rest aside from brief periods of sleeping. The only sustenance available were snacks and water, and I pushed myself to do what needed to be done."

"I don't know that I would fare well being in the military," Kendal admitted. "I've done some long shifts, but to have to work for two days straight and not know why I am doing it would be more than I think I could handle. I don't always like people telling me what to do."

Derek laughed. "I can attest to that."

She punched him in the arm. "Stop." She laughed and gave him a kiss.

Terry chuckled and continued. "The Marine Corps is clear about their expectations for enlisted members: they are there to serve the Corps. Officers are not likely to take the time to elaborate on why a certain order was given or what is required of you as an enlisted servicemember. The hierarchical system exists today and is maintained by the officers in charge, who set the plans and are in command.

"There's an old saying that goes, 'How does an officer put up a flagpole? Answer: "Sergeant, put up that flagpole!' Senior enlisted personnel know the reasons and details behind orders, but they don't typically go out of their way to explain it to enlisted members—it's just part of military tradition. The sooner you accept this fact, the easier your time will be in the Marines or any other branch of service."

Derek squeezed Kendal's hand. "I never even thought of going into the service. My life had pretty much been planned out for me. Plus, with all the extensive surgeries and repairs that had to be done to my body, I don't think they would have taken me anyway." Kendal squeezed his hand back, nodding with understanding.

"Given the lack of healthy communication, as well as the harsh words and negative outlook of the military lifestyle, it may seem like this would not be an ideal place to grow and develop. However, you'd be mistaken in such a conclusion." Terry took his cigar stub out of his mouth and took a swig of his beer, then stuck the cigar stub back.

"What takes place is the typical hardworking Marine, with their strong-willed disposition, looks for ways to do better in their assigned role. They strive to fit into the larger purpose of their command and put in immense effort to carry out the mission, obey orders, and help build up their group's strength and expertise. Rewards like medals and commendations are few and far between in the Corps, so you have to keep working hard no matter what."

Terry raised his hand to the barmaid, swirling it in the air indicating he was ready for another round of drinks.

"You come to take responsibility and be proud of the things you can do, within yourself, with your squad, in your unit, at your command, as a part of the Corps, and for your nation! It isn't immediate and not everyone achieves it.

"It is high, and it is even higher among those who serve in the military. This life is not easy; it takes both mental strength and physical stamina. That's why someone who has the title of 'Marine' carries it for life—there are no 'ex-Marines,' only Marines who have served or are currently serving, and we are always ready to serve in some capacity for the rest of our lives. Hoorah!"

Derek smiled with admiration at Terry, then lifted his glass and they all clinked them together in a toast.

"The dedication we feel to our Corps might be difficult for the average person to understand, but it comes from a sense of pride in what we have achieved and through being part of something larger than ourselves. As Marines, we know that we may lay down our lives, but by dedicating ourselves to service and loyalty, the Corps will never cease to exist, and neither will our country's way of life. We, with all other Marines before us, are forever a part of the United States Marine Corps!"

Terry grinned and lifted his glass. "The Marine Corps' motto is *Semper Fidelis*, a Latin phrase which translates to 'Always Faithful.'"

Chapter 17

Tyler stood in the center of the room, surrounded by that faint smell of sweat and leather. He had been training all week for this fight and knew this was the moment he had to be at his best. He had to draw from every reserve of strength and skill he had cultivated over the years and channel all of his focus into the task ahead. His brother's life depended on it. He closed his eyes and took a deep breath, letting it fill his lungs as he visualized the victory ahead.

Tyler had been preparing for the fight both mentally and physically, and now it was almost time for him to prove his worth.

He knew that the most stressful period would be waiting in the locker room, waiting for his fight and hearing the sounds of the crowd screaming, cheering, or booing.

He also knew that is what could break a fighter's spirit before they even got in the ring. Your mind starts to play tricks on you, and you start panicking, envisioning the worst scenarios, like getting beat up and knocked out. You're defeated before you even compete.

"The key is to focus your thoughts on your game plan," he told himself aloud. "The moves that you worked on in training, and the belief that no matter what your opponent throws at you, you can adapt and control the rhythm of the bout. Focus on being the master of the situation, and that you've trained hard and smart, and you are ready.

"Don't focus on getting a fast knockout, just to get it over with quickly—that can make you reckless and get you hit and hurt yourself. Focus on controlling the action, the rhythm of your opponent."

He started with a light workout, stretching his muscles and getting them warmed up in preparation. As he moved through each exercise, he felt his energy increasing, making him feel more alive than ever before. Excitement built within him, filling every inch of his being as he focused on what was to come. He knew that he was ready.

When he finished his workout, Tyler moved to the center of the room and began to visualize the fight ahead. He imagined himself performing each move flawlessly, executing every defense and attack with precision and skill. The visualization brought a wave of focus and determination over him.

Next, he moved into a meditative state, allowing himself to clear his mind and focus all of his attention on the present moment. He let go of all worries and distractions, and embraced the calmness that was slowly washing over him. He found his center and took a few moments to steady himself before ending the meditation.

When he opened his eyes, Tyler felt a sense of peace and balance. He knew that if he had to step into the ring, he would be ready for whatever came his way. He exhaled deeply and smiled, feeling confident and energized. He was ready for the fight for his brother's life.

Derek moved around the house quietly, barely making a sound. His mind was in a state of intense concentration, as if he were trying to piece together a complex puzzle. All the necessary components for the night's event were in his possession. Everything had to be perfectly in place in order for Derek's mission to succeed. The weight of the responsibility for these two young men's safety bore down hard on him; their lives were in his hands.

Derek, Tyler, and Terry had been preparing for this moment all week, and although it felt like they'd been running against the clock, Derek hoped they had everything in order.

"This is nerve-wracking," Tyler said. "I have always trained hard, but nothing can ever prepare me for a real fight in front of people. Especially since so much is riding on it with my brother. My nerves and adrenaline have been overwhelming. I have had to meditate continuously to keep them under control."

"You've trained hard," Derek reassured him. "I know you feel a lot of pressure to perform, especially because you are worried about your brother's safety. On top of not knowing what to expect from your opponent, I am sure it can be anxiety-inducing. Take it from me, you have to control your nerves and fight through them."

"Yeah, but if you haven't experienced it, you don't know how it is when you hear the crowd and the bell goes off for the first round," Tyler replied grimly. "It can be startling. It causes your body to tense up involuntarily. I have to remind myself to relax and fight."

Derek nodded. "Look at it this way: with all the training, you finally get to test your skills against a real opponent. There is a thrill to that. Seeing and hearing the crowd cheer can boost your energy and motivate you to perform. As the match gets going, you will settle into a rhythm, the excitement will take over, and your nerves will fade. When you win, *and you will win*, the feeling of accomplishment and joy for setting your brother free will be indescribable. I know this is a nerve-wracking test for you. But you can also view it as an exciting rite of passage that you will remember forever."

With quiet deliberation, Derek selected the right pieces of clothing for the evening's events and set them in a neat pile on his dresser. The time had come. He needed to take a break, if only for a few moments, and decided to ride over to see Terry. Derek wasn't sure he was ready even though he had convinced Tyler he was. Had they done all the work they could do to prepare? He put his hand on the doorknob to the living room and took a deep breath, anxiety rushing through his body. He opened the door and silently left the penthouse, making sure it was locked behind him.

The sun was bright, the air fresh, as he rode his Harley out of the underground garage. It was one of those days that just made you feel alive, a feeling that the leather and chrome of the bike amplified. He had been cooped up inside all morning worrying about what was about to happen, so the sudden burst of wind was a welcome surprise, blowing the cobwebs from his brain.

Terry's tattoo parlor stood out like a beacon on the main street of the little beach town. A brightly lit sign above the entrance proclaimed, *Tattoos by appointment only*. As Derek walked up to the door, his heart began to beat faster. He was nervous, but he reminded himself that helping Tyler free his brother was something he had chosen to do.

He knew that it was important for him to take control and create a path for helping other people. His thoughts had been focused on stressful and worrisome events of late, and these major triggers made it easy to get into a pattern of negative self-talk and revert back to thinking only of himself.

He took a deep breath and grabbed the door handle, the cool metal against his palm grounding him. A chime sounded as Derek entered the parlor. The walls were adorned with familiar artworks of tattoos in different styles and sizes. The shop smelled like incense and leather; it was quiet yet inviting.

Derek paused in the doorway, taking in all the details. He could see Terry through the bead curtain in the back, engrossed in his work. He barely glanced up when Derek entered, seemingly expecting him. Derek felt his anxiety dissipating, replaced by a feeling of determination and assurance. Just being around a strong leadership personality like Terry made him feel more confident. Derek was there to make sure he was prepared and ready.

Terry finally came out from behind the beads. He wore a military-style camo cap and tight camo T-shirt that hugged his fit middle-aged body. He pulled the cigar stub from his mouth and called out in his usual raspy voice, "Hey, Doc, how are you doing today?"

"Just checking in." Derek felt his anxiety mount again; he knew they were all putting themselves in danger, with a chance of getting hurt or worse. "I thought we'd spend some time coordinating the plan. We've got lots to do and not much time to do it."

Terry struck a power pose, legs apart. "I already went over everything with my guys. I also spoke to the LAPD, and they are going to be staking out the event tonight. They're working a couple of cases, so they'll have eyes watching for our boy." He put one hand on his hip. "He's not leaving with ZhiZhu tonight."

"That makes me feel a whole lot better." Derek's spirits lifted, but he knew there was still plenty that could go wrong. He started to pace, staring at the floor and working through what Terry had told him.

"We just need to make sure that we get our hands on Tyler quickly before the crowd disperses, or no one is going to be able to help." Terry's calm gaze tracked Derek's strides back and forth across the room. "Do you know where he is on the fight card?" Terry knew the answer but needed to make sure Derek was also prepared.

Derek stopped in midstep and looked up. "Second to last. That's why it's critical to get this done fast. If the fight before his is a short one, we could get caught up in the crowd, and then we're back in the same place, negotiating all over again."

Terry nodded in agreement. "Once Tyler wins his fight, then we must make the exchange. Where should that happen?"

Terry knew they had to get the details right and he needed Derek to say it out loud. To confirm he knew how it was all going to work.

Derek continued thinking. "Well, *if he fights*, there are three five-minute rounds with a minute in between. Once the fight starts, all men and vehicles need to be in a position to extradite the boys." Derek knew he had to get the synchronization down.

"*After the fight*, take him directly out of the ring," Terry instructed. "Do not go back to the locker room." Terry had spent the evening studying the layout. "There is an exit door to the left of the hall, head straight for that door. I will have a man standing there to take you out to the vehicle." He put the cigar stub back in his mouth.

Derek's subconscious pacing continued. "What about his brother?" He stopped. He could feel his toes squeeze together tightly; he was getting a cramp in his damned foot. "And the money?" He bounced on one foot trying to make the cramp release.

Terry frowned as he watched him bounce. "We'll have eyes on Tyler's brother." Terry could feel the unnecessary energy coming from

Derek's pacing. He snapped his fingers in front of Derek to get his attention. "When the fight is over . . ." He spoke slowly, "We'll make the exchange quickly. No money will swap hands until we have Jason. It will all happen simultaneously."

"What about Tyler?" Derek felt compelled to be hypervigilant. "He wanted to be there."

Terry pulled the cigar stub from his mouth. "*Tyler doesn't get to be there.* This is going to go down very fast. The only thing he needs to understand is what is expected of him. Tell him to do his part and let us worry about the rest. Once we have everyone secured in the vehicles, we will meet back at my place. Do you understand?"

Derek frowned. "He's worried about something going wrong, that his brother might get hurt."

Terry adjusted the cap on his head, trying to stay patient. He wasn't used to someone talking back to him. In an even tone of voice, he explained, "The only thing that I can see that's going to be a challenge is if Tyler loses. So, we need to be prepared for anything to keep the advantage. Here's how it's going to go down."

He spoke precisely and clearly. "If for some reason Tyler *does lose*, or this is all just a set-up . . . because face it, they may be betting that he is going to lose," he squinted at Derek, "then they will try to keep his brother for another deal and more money."

Refusing to accept the possibility of failure, Derek said firmly, "Tyler is not going to lose."

Terry slowly shook his head. "Well, you never know what these guys are up to. They could drug him, or the other guy could do something to incapacitate him." Terry watched Derek's reaction. "There are many tricks of the trade that they could pull off to throw this fight. Just stay on your toes."

Terry needed to make sure Derek understood. He took a step closer to look him dead in the eye. "If he loses, the course is the same. Head back toward the locker room as quickly as possible, but then make the quick left to the exit door where my guy will be waiting."

They remained in an eye-lock.

"Do you understand?" he growled.

"What about his brother?" Derek repeated the question.

"We'll have him in our sights," Terry reassured Derek, "that's all you need to know. If they throw the fight or we lose the fight, we are prepared to take him anyway."

"Oh, man." He exhaled a breath and ran his hand across the back of his neck. "This isn't going to turn into a shootout or something, is it?"

"No, it shouldn't," Terry replied in a firm voice, "but we will be ready if it does."

Terry had seen men like this before. Derek had that thousand-yard stare that Terry recognized from his tours of duty. In the heat of battle, it was easy for men to start to come apart. They had to have a plan. A sense that their actions mattered and were part of something bigger.

Terry took a deep breath and slowly started to explain the strategy they had discussed only hours before. He reminded Derek of the plan, how they had to trust it, and to not take any risks that could endanger the boys. He spoke calmly and evenly, looking into Derek's eyes as he did so. When he was done, Derek nodded, though Terry wasn't quite sure he had taken in any of the information he was just given.

Derek went back to pacing nervously. He shoved one hand in his pocket and started twisting the motorcycle key.

"Listen, just focus on Tyler." Terry pinpointed Derek's specific duty for the mission. "Keep him safe by making sure he gets in the ring and fights. That's all we need, nothing more. The rest is being handled, got it?"

Derek stopped, looking up. "Yeah, I do." There was nothing more for him to do than to carry out the mission to save these boys from the drug lords.

"Good. I'll see you over there tonight at eight. Try to stay calm and keep Tyler calm. The last thing we need is for him to go rogue on us."

"I got it." Derek reached out to shake Terry's hand.

Terry took his hand and squeezed. "Hang in there, buddy, this will be over soon."

Terry had demonstrated he was battle-ready. That everything was under control. He had responded specifically to each of Derek's questions. They would have to rely on careful planning, divine providence, and a bit of good fortune to get through the situation.

Terry gave Derek a reassuring pat on the shoulder and watched as he walked out the door, listening to the exhaust sound of his motorcycle leaving.

Derek adjusted his helmet and revved the engine, feeling the power of the machine between his legs. As he rode away from the tattoo shop and out onto the open road, he felt the trepidation melt away and an influx of exhilaration as he took in the sights and smells of the ocean. This time of year, the wildflowers were in full bloom alongside the road. The fresh scent of grass wafted its way up into his helmet. He felt a semblance of peace—a feeling that he knew was fleeting but savored all the same.

With the wind in his face, he imagined he was riding toward an unknown destination, if only in his mind, his future unclear but with the promise of something exciting ahead of him. He opened up the throttle and felt the thrill of the acceleration as the pavement flew by beneath him. He knew the mission to help these young men get out of trouble would present a challenge, but he was ready for whatever came next.

Chapter 18

All day, time seemed to move in reverse for Tyler. He kept looking at the clock, counting down how long before he would have to get ready and leave for the fight club—and the fight itself.

Tyler and Derek arrived at The Lodge in Studio City at a couple of minutes before eight. A waiting car pulled out of the strategically located parking space for them to pull in, just as Terry had instructed. At the entrance ramp, ZhiZhu's men patted them down for weapons and then led them to a side door.

They followed a man down a long hallway with a series of doors. The air as they passed the locker rooms was heavy with anticipation as the fighters prepared for their entrances. A certain electricity seemed to pulse through the rooms, a mixture of fear and excitement that fueled them for the upcoming battles.

Their escort stopped to open a door. Inside a locker room, seated on a bench, was a man dressed in an expensive tuxedo—ZhiZhu.

Tyler and Derek stepped in and scanned the room. Two other men stood against the wall.

"There's my Magic Monk!" ZhiZhu laughed. "I've been waiting for you."

When the door closed, the two men didn't move. They watched Tyler with flat, sharklike eyes.

"Well, let's get to it. Don't you have to start warming up or something?" ZhiZhu asked.

Tyler walked past ZhiZhu and opened a locker. Putting his workout bag on the bench, he started to undress. Derek tried to mask his frustration.

"Listen, ZhiZhu, how do you expect him to concentrate on the fight if you're in here messing with his head and causing unnecessary tension in the room?"

"Me?" He locked eyes on Tyler. "I'm here for support."

"Well, now you've shown him your support, we should give him a couple minutes to concentrate so he can get ready for the fight."

"You know, when this is done, I might just want to pop that smart mouth of yours," ZhiZhu said, pointing his index finger with thumb up like a gun muzzle at Derek's head.

"Remember our agreement, ZhiZhu," Derek said in a calm, slow voice, making sure there was no miscommunication. "I'm just suggesting that he be given some time to get ready."

"No problem. We want our Magic Monk to have all his powers intact." He reached over to touch a tattoo on Tyler's back.

Tyler jumped and tensed like a caged animal being teased. Derek launched his body between them before Tyler tore ZhiZhu apart.

"Now that is what I like to see. The fire! Now go tear him up," ZhiZhu teased. He motioned for one of his guys to open the door. "Remember little brother is counting on you," he winked.

It was obvious that his annoying behavior had been meant to throw Tyler off his game. The three men walked out, and the door closed.

Tyler collapsed onto the bench. "I don't know if I can do this."

"Of course, you can. Don't be nervous." Derek put his hand on his shoulder. "Just go out there and spar." Derek could feel his hand give a slight tremble. He removed it immediately. Tyler needed him now more than ever.

Derek heard the words in his head of his kickboxing instructor before a match, and parroted them back to Tyler. "Once you get in the ring to fight, your nerves will vanish. The fight itself will seem like a blur. You don't have time to think—you react, you're on autopilot.

"You have trained and sparred extensively and understand what being in a combat-sport situation is. You've programmed yourself for success. You are in top physical condition. You are mentally and spiritually prepared."

Tyler looked Derek in the eye. "This is more than sparring. That guy out there is going to try to kill me by any means within his power."

Derek held his gaze. "Then go out there and utilize your intelligence. Fight smarter, not harder. Pick your shots. Keep yourself safe by avoiding throwing unnecessary punches." Derek heard his own mentor's voice. "Throw the right strikes at the right times. Leverage your knowledge . . . capitalize on your experience."

He stood up to pace. "You're a thinker. Be patient. Wait for your opponent's mistakes, land key shots," he unleashed a couple of air punches, "avoid taking on too much damage, and you can rack up the points."

"I know I have the skill, it's what's in my heart when I go out there . . ."

"Keep your focus." Derek squatted down in front of Tyler, who sat on the bench. "Be merciful but with an undeniable will to win. Be relentless and fight to the finish. You are doing the right thing. Don't think about anything else." He gave him a pat on the knee and stood back up.

"Thanks." Tyler stood to wrap one gloved hand around the back of Derek's neck. "I appreciate you being here."

Tyler knew most fighters got nervous before a fight, but this wasn't just *any fight*. The difference between winning and losing would be the difference between life and death. Control could only come with experience and practice. He sat back down on the bench. Derek leaned against a locker and watched in silence.

To overcome his pre-fight nerves, Tyler closed his eyes then started his relaxation techniques. He started with visualization to improve his performance, manage anxiety, and develop his confidence. He knew this technique would implement his experienced mental triggers.

To prepare himself for the almost intolerable task at hand, he felt his body relax as he focused on his breath, the steady rhythm calming his racing heart. He imagined himself in the ring, ready to deliver a stunning knock-out punch.

Suddenly, the room seemed to stretch out around him, and he was in the moment, ready to fight. All outside noise and distractions drifted away, and Tyler was left with his thoughts and his determination. He was ready. He was focused. He was prepared to take on anything that came his way.

A rap on the door. "Ten minutes," boomed the voice.

Tyler started his warmup routine by jogging in place, feet lightly hitting the floor. He felt alive and energized, taking deep breaths as his feet moved in a steady rhythm. Then he performed a sweeping round-house kick that could deliver a devastating strike used in combat sports.

Derek continued to lean against the locker and simply observe. With his limited experience in martial arts, he was filled with admiration.

The Muay Thai roundhouse kick is thrown like a baseball bat, unlike kicks from martial arts like karate which land with a snap. This attack requires the body to generate momentum to increase its force. The power of the roundhouse made Tyler spin around completely.

As his breath gradually deepened, the sound of his own breath soothed him.

Arms swinging in sync with the jogging, he stretched out further until he could touch his toes. From there he moved on to lunges, feeling his leg muscles contract and release. He pushed himself with a few more repetitions.

Next came the squats, feeling the weight of his body and the strain in his glutes as he went lower and lower. Finally, he was ready, and with a deep exhale he rose to standing. He felt limber, strong, and prepared.

Outside, Terry walked around the boxing ring, looking through the crowd of the stadium-style seating of The Lodge. The atmosphere started to change as the hardcore fans came early. People shuffled in, their footsteps muffled by the buzz of conversation. As the seats filled up, the tension in the air became palpable. It was as if the entire audience had money riding on the fights and was holding its breath, waiting for the unknown. The crowd had reached capacity in the auditorium.

The anticipation grew louder with each passing second, until finally, the lights dimmed, and the first fight was announced. The noise level rose and fell like a wave, as fans chanted their favorite fighter's name and waved flags or signs in support. The audience collectively leaned forward, eager to see what was about to unfold.

The tension was palpable, and every person in the building could feel it. They knew they were about to witness a display of physical prowess and determination, a battle of wills and skills. All eyes were fixed on the corridor, watching for the fighters to emerge from their locker rooms and make their entrances.

When the first fighter's name was announced, he emerged from his locker room, his face stoic and focused. He walked with purpose down the corridor, the cameras tracking his every movement. As he stepped into the arena's bright lights, the electricity in the air intensified, crackling with energy. The first fight of the evening was about to begin, and the crowd was hungry for action. The fighters, two muscular men with fierce determination in their eyes, stood in their respective corners, awaiting the start of the match.

The crowd erupted into cheers and applause when the first fighter took his place in the center of the ring, ready to face his opponent. The moment of truth had arrived, and everyone held their breath, waiting for the first punch to be thrown.

Suddenly, the bell rang out, signaling the start of the fight. The two men charged at each other, fists flying and bodies colliding with a loud thud. The spectators roared as the fight intensified, their shouts and screams blending into a chaotic symphony. The audience jumped to its feet, cheering and shouting as if they were the ones in the ring. Every punch, dodge, and kick was met with a visceral response from the crowd, who were fully invested in the fight's outcome. It was a primal reaction, an instinctual response to the display of strength and skill. And as the fights continued, the crowd remained hyped, their energy never waning as they cheered on their favorite fighters. They were caught up in the moment, swept away by the intensity of the experience.

Terry walked around the boxing ring, looking through the crowd until he spied Tyler's brother, Jason, seated with two men in the arena. It appeared that he was not being held captive but seemed to be just hanging out. Terry watched as one man gave the other a fist bump. They were standing up the whole time, smoking weed right in front of everyone. He moved in closer to keep his eye on the men.

One seemed like he was pretty deeply involved in the fight business. Terry moved in closer and overheard him explain how he had ties to several of the good fighters. He seemed knowledgeable and mentioned how common fixed fights were in the sport. This confirmed what Terry had been thinking—that this would be a no-win situation for Tyler.

The crowd buzzed with anticipation as they waited for the next fight to begin. Terry continued to observe Tyler's brother with the men and their behavior, quickly snapping photos with his phone when they were distracted.

The noise was almost deafening. The smell of sweat and adrenaline filled the air, permeating the arena and adding to the charged atmosphere. As the next fighter made his way to the ring, the crowd erupted into a wall of clapping. Tyler's brother continued to chill with his two supposed "captors." Everyone was on their feet, transfixed by the spectacle before them. The sound was like thunder, a loud roar that filled the space.

The crowd remained hyped during the first few fights. In between rounds, the low hum of conversation overlapped with the occasional shout or cheer. It was a cool night, but the bodies packed tightly together generated enough warmth to make the air feel heavy and humid. Some spectators were dressed in their finest, others in their work clothes. Regardless of their appearance, all eyes were fixed on the ring in the center of the room.

As the fight went on, it was clear that this was no ordinary brawl. Both fighters were skilled and relentless, each landing powerful blows and refusing to back down. It was a battle of strength, endurance, and pure willpower. As the final blow was delivered, knocking one of the fighters to the ground, Jason leaped from his seat in celebration with the roar of the crowd.

The fighter in the ring raised his arms in victory, his chest heaving as he took in the cheers and applause. By this time Terry had seen enough. It was time to report back to Tyler what he had observed.

This new development was going to present a problem. It hadn't occurred to Terry when he had run all the scenarios that Tyler's brother didn't want to be rescued and that he might put up resistance. Terry marched quickly back to the locker room; he saw a man standing outside the door. Thinking quickly, he gave the hand signal for one of his guys to approach from the opposite direction to distract the guard long enough for him to slip into the room.

Terry opened the locker-room door and quickly slipped in, startling Tyler and Derek.

"What are you doing here?" Derek asked in a hushed voice. "How did you get in? You're supposed to be out front."

"I'm aware," Terry replied gruffly. "We need to have a chat."

Derek frowned. His gut told him something was wrong. "What's going on?"

Terry crinkled his eyes. "Tyler's brother is not a prisoner. He's hanging out with them. It looks like he's part of whatever is going on. I'm not sure. But he's hanging out and partying with two of the guys, like long-lost pals or something. What do you want us to do?"

Tyler's jaw tensed. "No, he wouldn't do that to me," he growled through flared nostrils.

"Well, take a look." Terry pulled out his phone and flipped through the photos.

"I'll kill him." Tyler punched the locker.

"No," Derek said softly, "we can't worry about that right now."

"Okay, let's think here." Terry stepped back and put his phone back in his pocket.

"I'm not going out there to fight for a scam my brother is pulling!" Tyler wrapped his arms around his bare torso. "They almost got you to fork over a hundred grand," he groaned.

"We have to figure out how to get out of here without anyone getting hurt." Terry thought through the memorized escape routes. "Let's still go out the side door." He pulled his phone out again. "I'll tell my guys to abort."

"What if this is all a setup to make it look like Jason is working with them?" Tyler's mind was racing. "They could have planned this to deceive us. To trick us into thinking he's guilty of doing something wrong.

"Go out and take a look for yourself." Terry walked over and put his hand on the door handle. "When you head out to the ring, look to the center of the room, he's sitting with two guys. If you want to fight, move forward to the ring. If not, head to the exit, the car will be right outside. I'll wait until you walk out and then slip out right behind you." He opened the door stood back to let them go out first.

Tyler and Derek stepped out into the hallway. The man guarding the door moved forward to walk behind them. Terry had slipped past unnoticed in the opposite direction. Tyler exited the hallway into the arena, then scanned the room to find his younger brother. Chanting fans, hooligans, and a raucous and festive atmosphere made the place vibrate with energy. They laughed, booed and cheered like fight crowds anywhere.

For the size of the room, the crowd seemed pretty large. The place was packed to capacity. The midlevel tickets where Tyler's brother sat had him jammed in like a sardine, but that didn't seem to hamper his enthusiasm.

Derek and Tyler stood in the aisle and had a perfect view of all the action. They could hear the blows. The ringside tables held people pretending to be big shots or supporting a fighter on the card. In the front row, close to the fighters slugging, blood splattered onto the spectators. This was much more brutal than Derek could ever have imagined.

The body shots seemed much more devastating in person as Derek stood watching the fight. The slightest hint of a possible knockout seemed to get everyone out of their seats. The crowd was aggressive, and pumped for an altercation, with fights breaking out intermittently throughout the stands. Most people seemed to be drunk or on some type of substance. The hairs on Derek's arms rose up like needles; it felt like they were standing on a powder keg about to blow. His eyes fixed on the stage, but his mind was elsewhere. He couldn't shake off the feeling that something bad was about to happen.

Tyler continued to scan the room; then he saw Jason seated in the middle of the row, laughing and drinking. It was apparent he was not under any duress. Tyler's heart sank.

"We are going for the exit." Tyler mumbled, staring out into the crowd.

Derek paused to analyze the situation. It felt like an eternity as they stood out in the middle of the floor exposed. "Are you sure?"

Mystified by his brother's behavior, he replied, "Yeah, I'm sure."

He could see Terry standing in a corner. Being careful to keep his voice low, Derek barely moved his lips. "Okay, when they announce the winner of this fight and everybody stands up, let's make our move."

People stood everywhere along the perimeter of the room, even in the back, blocking the exit. It would be tough to work their way through the crowd. Derek was glad they were supposed to go out the side exit, so they could make their way along the wall. As soon as the announcer started to call the fight, he said in a loud whisper, "Let's take this guy down." He and Tyler turned in unison and pushed the man back into the hall. Overtaking him, they knocked him out. Then they made their way out the side exit to where the strategically parked car waited.

Back at the penthouse, Tyler was distraught. He knew with utter certainty that he had been bamboozled. His brother had officially broken his heart.

"I can't believe I involved all of you. I jeopardized other people's lives and finances. I feel like such a fool." Tyler knew he had a lapse in judgment and was furious with himself.

"Listen, that's what we do when we love somebody," Derek said firmly. "We all underestimated him. How were you supposed to know? We don't blame you. You believed him. It's your brother who's responsible for putting us all in danger. He rejected your support and abandoned his responsibilities just to pursue his personal gratification."

Tyler's cellphone rang. He looked at the screen. "It's my brother. I don't think I can talk to him."

"I will." Derek took the phone from Tyler. "Hello?"

"Who's this?" the voice barked.

"Tatman," Derek barked back.

"I need to talk to my brother. Put him on."

"He's pretty broken up right now, Jason, he doesn't want to talk."

"He has to listen to me. If he doesn't give me that money," his voice made a choking sound, "I'm a dead man."

"Maybe you are and maybe you aren't. But you didn't look too concerned tonight when you were drinking and smoking with your buddies."

"That's because I had to play along," Jason whined.

In a flat tone, Derek said, "It's over." He looked at Tyler, sitting on the couch, head in hand.

"Put my brother on." The tone changed to anger.

"He's not going to fall for it anymore, Jason."

Jason's voice deepened. "You know I can make you disappear, right?"

"No, you can't make me disappear. You better talk to your boss about that one. I took out insurance. Your boss and I have a mutual trust and now you've broken that trust. Tell your boss that I am going to have to think about what our next step is going to be." Derek ended the call.

Tyler sat on the couch, rubbing his head. "I feel sick. He just threatened you?"

"You and me both," Derek confirmed. "It's a shame you have to go through this. But better you find out now before you fought in the ring and we gave them the money."

"Look what he's put us all through." He ran his fingers through his hair, pulling at the roots.

"Your brother has fallen. It's obvious he's in deep. I'm sure he's addicted. Why would he go to such lengths?"

"Yeah, you're right."

"I would disappear and not let him know where you are. And I would warn your mom," Derek suggested.

"I can't just walk away and let him throw his life down the drain like that." Tyler's eyes began to well up again.

"Believe me, you don't have any say about it right now. Drug addiction is powerful. Look what he just did. It took a lot of thought, desire, and motivation for him to pull this off. You can't fight against that. You're going to have to wait until he comes to a point where he's willing to change."

Tyler shook his head. "I don't know if that will ever happen."

"He's the only one that can make that decision. For you to try to change him would only be enabling him and ruining your own life. The best thing you can do is to let him know that you love him and will always love him, but you can never accept his destructive behavior." Derek hung his head; he could feel his own disappointment and grief.

Tyler took a deep breath, then sighed. "Thanks, Doc. You have been a blessing to me. I don't know what would have happened without having you and Terry with me. I could have been sucked into all of it."

Derek looked at him and felt true compassion. "That's my point. Don't let your life be ruined. You could have been hurt or killed, all for another high. Life is worthless to these people. They worship the drugs, money, and power, and they don't care who they destroy to get it."

"I see that now—and they have taken my brother down with them." Tyler leaned back and crossed his arms.

"They couldn't have taken your brother if he hadn't chosen to go with them." Derek stood looking out the window at the horizon. "He might be a prisoner now because of his habit, but I can guarantee you that he has had plenty of opportunities to get out along the way. People do not get in that deep into an organization without doing some crazy things to get there. And look what he was willing to do to you."

"I know you're right. It's just hard to walk away."

Derek turned from the window. "You're not the one walking away. He did, a long time ago, when he made the decision to get involved with drugs and criminals. There's no reason for you to feel guilty about this. He chose the path."

"I should have stayed here and taken care of him." Tyler let out a sob.

"How do you know that if you had stayed here that he wouldn't have taken the same path? If the excitement of drugs is so tantalizing, then you would have sacrificed your future only to have him throw it all away." Derek walked over to stand in front of Tyler. "You aren't his parent. You said, yourself, he was already heading in that direction before you left. You would have been one more person he resented. Instead, now he looks at you as possibly having the answers to his problems."

Derek sat down in the chair next to Tyler. "So, don't let him misuse you. Let him know you want to help him into a better life but not that way. Tell him that you will be there for him when he is ready to get on the right track."

"I don't think he's going to listen, but I think it's a good idea." Tyler wiped the tears from his face.

"Of course, he's not going to listen. Not right now. But make it your mantra. Every time you talk to him say, 'I am here for you when you are ready to start your life fresh. I love you.' Keep it simple. Don't preach. Try to keep him coming back to hear the message."

"I think I understand where you are going with this." Tyler nodded.

"It's not going to be easy. You're going to see some bizarre behavior. But you have your faith, and you're solid in your beliefs, now you know why you went through what you did. So, you can be there for him. To fight for him. Right? Try to give him little tidbits of wisdom each time to draw him closer to you. Give him messages of love and acceptance. Not of his lifestyle but of him as a person and a brother."

"Thank you, Doc, I really don't know how I would be handling this by myself."

"I'm glad that I've been able to be here for you."

Tyler got up slowly and left the room.

Despite the late hour, Derek decided to give Kendal a quick call to update her on the evening's events. He knew she would be worried.

Chapter 19

Arriving early, Derek was apprehensive about Ami Soo showing up to the office for her next treatment after what had gone down with her brother the night before. He and Kendal sat in his office nervously waiting.

"I sure hope they don't show up with guns or something." Kendal stared at Derek across the desk.

"They aren't going to do that," Derek said. "Remember, I have information on them." He turned his chair to look out the window, feeling the weight of her gaze on the back of his neck.

Derek knew that he had the upper hand, but also that he would need to be careful how he played it. He was prepared to act with force, if necessary, but he hoped it wouldn't come to that.

"But wasn't that if the original deal went down?" Kendal reminded him.

"That was based on mutual trust." He turned back to look her in the eye. "ZhiZhu obviously didn't hold up his end of the bargain when he tried to deceive us about their relationship. He made it sound like he was holding Jason for ransom when Jason has been working for them all along."

They jumped as the chime to the front door of the office sounded. Kendal's eyes widened. They both got up from their chairs to go out to the front; Derek took hold of her arm. "Let me go first."

At the front desk Ami Soo stood waiting with a young girl.

"Ami Soo, so nice to see you again." Derek smiled.

"Hello." Ami Soo's face remained weirdly blank.

"Come on back." Derek ignored the odd response and motioned for the girls to follow him to the nearest exam room. Kendal waited by the door to assist.

"I am going to have you change in here, and then we are going to go over to where the laser is. Leave your clothes on except your top, put this on." Kendal handed Ami Soo a hospital gown. She looked over at the other young woman. The girl remained silent and put her head down, avoiding eye contact.

Derek looked at Kendal and shrugged. "Okay, we will be back in a couple minutes to take you for your procedure."

After setting up the equipment in the laser room, Kendal went back to get Ami Soo. She knocked on the door and opened it to find the young girl folding her blouse. It struck Kendal as odd. The girl kept her head down and backed away to sit back on the chair.

"Okay, Ami Soo. We are ready for you. Your friend can wait here for you."

"Oh, she's not my friend. She works for my brother. My boyfriend insisted that she come today to take care of me," she said with a frown.

"Okay, well then what is her name?" Kendal watched the young girl's face as they spoke.

"Marie—that is what we call her. I don't know if that's the name her parents gave her."

"What's her last name?"

"I don't know."

"How old is she?"

"I don't know."

"Where does she come from?"

"I'm really not sure." She crossed her arms. "We think she's Spanish, from South America someplace. I think she came to my brother for a job, and he took her in. She would have starved on the streets." Ami Soo jutted her chin out. "My brother is very generous when it comes to giving people jobs."

"Um, I'm sure he is." Kendal furrowed her eyebrows. "Well let's get you to the laser room. Dr. Hollinger is waiting. Marie, you can wait here for Ami Soo. This won't take too long, okay?"

The girl didn't even look up.

"She doesn't understand you." Ami Soo looked at Marie and wrinkled her nose. "We have a guy who tells her what my brother wants her to know in Spanish."

Kendal nodded but felt a heaviness in her heart for Marie as she led Ami Soo to the surgery room.

Derek and Kendal performed the second treatment on Ami Soo. During the procedure, Marie's face kept running through Kendal's mind. Something was not right. Derek finished the treatment and Kendal immediately excused herself.

She walked quickly back to the room where Marie was waiting. When Kendal opened the door, the girl jumped like a rabbit.

"Marie, I'm Kendal, it's okay."

The girl sat back in the chair and hung her head.

"Marie, where are you from?"

She didn't move or say anything.

Kendal moved in closer. "Marie, are you okay?"

No answer.

Kendal crouched down to look her directly in the eye. "Marie, do you understand me? Marie, *hablas ingles*?"

The young girl met her gaze for the first time, her face bearing the unmistakable marks of fear and uncertainty. "No," she said, her voice barely more than a whisper.

"Oh, okay." Kendal smiled and returned to the surgery in time to help Derek assist Ami Soo off the table.

"I'm going to show you how to apply the aftercare medicine." Kendal picked up a jar that sat on the counter.

"Can you show Marie as well?" Ami Soo asked.

"Of course." Kendal guided Ami Soo by the arm back to the examining room.

After Kendal gave Marie the skin care demonstration, Ami Soo made the next appointment and confirmed that Angel was waiting downstairs. The two girls left together.

"Well, that went better than expected," Derek said as they left the lobby. "Maybe her brother still doesn't know."

Derek turned to go back to his office, and Kendal followed him down the hall. "They know what went down at the fight arena last night," she said. "They just haven't connected the dots yet."

"That's certainly possible." Derek sat back down heavily into his chair. "So, let's keep our fingers crossed we can get this done before ZhiZhu finds out."

"Well, how do you think that's going to happen?" Kendal sat down in one of the chairs in front of his desk and flipped her hair back. "The first time he sees Ami Soo, he is going to notice she doesn't have a birthmark."

"Hopefully she has a good story to tell him." Derek's lips curled to the side.

"You know that girl that was with her, Marie? I have a weird feeling about her." Kendal got up from her chair and started to pace. "Ami Soo told me that she works for her brother. This girl looks like she's maybe fourteen or fifteen at the most—and she works for her brother? She doesn't speak any English. They brought her over here from South America and treat her more like a little slave girl than an employee." Kendal shook her head. "I don't like it."

"What are you thinking?" Derek watched her as she walked from one side of the office to the other.

"I don't know. Let's see if they come back. We need to be able to talk to her." She stopped in midstride and looked at Derek. "Do you know anyone that speaks Spanish?"

Derek shrugged. "Cecelia, my housekeeper, but she is still not talking to me after the incident in my apartment when she saw me that first morning when I woke up covered in tattoos. I scared her, and I didn't handle it well when I just ran off."

"I can call her, maybe she'd be willing to come over to the office for their next appointment. We can kill two birds with one stone—talk to the girl and you can make up with Cecelia." Kendal smiled. "I'm sure your place needs a good cleaning by now."

"Yes, I guess it does. Plus, I miss seeing her, she's been with me for so many years. She is the only person that I still have a connection with who knew Dr. Casey."

"Okay, perfect. Let's give her a call and see what she says." Kendal held her hand out.

"Now?" He dug out his cellphone.

Kendal scrolled through his contact list until she came to the housekeeper's name. "Cecelia, hello. This is Kendal, Dr. Hollinger's manager. How are you?"

"Fine?" Cecelia's voice sounded weak.

"Dr. Hollinger asked me to call you to see if you would be willing to come into his office and talk to him." Kendal stared at Derek as she spoke.

"Now?" The housekeeper sounded tense. "To see him?"

"Yes. He would like you to come into his office and talk to him." Kendal smiled at Derek.

"Why?"

Kendal could hear the skepticism in her voice. "Because he would like to apologize for the misunderstanding he had with you at his penthouse."

"I do not want to see him," she said flatly.

"He looks much better," Kendal said in a light tone, winking at Derek.

"No more markings?"

Kendal turned to pace the office again. "Well, he still has the markings but not so many."

"Why does he have the markings?"

She looked back at Derek's face. "We don't know."

"I do," Cecelia said in a grim voice. "*El Diablo*."

"No, I don't think it's the devil." Kendal shook her head.

"Yes, in my country El Diablo does this."

Kendal shot a quick glance to Derek. "You've seen this before?"

"Yes. When I was a child."

"Who did you see that was covered in markings?" Kendal walked closer to Derek so he could hear what she was saying. She pressed the speaker button on the phone and set it on the desk.

"It was the Day of the Dead," Cecilia recounted in a fearful, hesitant voice. "My madre was working late and had left me home with my sisters and brothers. We were very scared because this is the day we go to the cemetery to leave food on the altar for the dead. By the time my mother came home it was late, but we went to the cemetery anyway. It was quiet, most of the people had gone home. When we left our offering, a large man walked up, covered in markings, and removed the offering from the altar."

Kendal's eyes grew wide. "That must have frightened you."

"Yes, my mother said that he was one of the walking dead."

"Well, now I understand why you are afraid of Dr. Hollinger, but believe me, he is not one of the walking dead, and he does not have anything to do with the devil. In fact, he has been seeing a priest who had been helping him try to find out why this has happened to him." She stared Derek in the eyes. "Plus, if you will take a couple of minutes to talk to him, I promise that I will be here as well."

"You will be there?"

Kendal picked the phone up off the desk. "Yes."

There was a brief pause. "Okay."

Kendal walked back around to the front of the desk. "When can you come by?"

"I just finished cleaning a house. I can stop by on my way home."

Kendal looked up and smiled. "That would be perfect. Thank you, Cecelia."

A little while later, the chime went off in the front office. Kendal went to the office's reception area to greet Cecelia. Kendal was a natural when it came to making patients feel comfortable and welcome. She did the same for Cecelia, offering her hand to the middle-aged woman with a soft, tan face. Cecilia smiled nervously and took Kendal's hand.

They walked together, but Cecelia proceeded with a wariness that was unmistakable. Kendal escorted her down the hall to Derek's office. Her feet moved slowly, and her gaze swept the empty rooms as they passed each door. She looked as if she had entered a haunted ruin.

Derek stood up when they entered his office. He tried to appear relaxed. "Hello, Cecelia."

Cecelia stepped back so fast she bumped into Kendal, who was standing behind her.

Kendal put her hands on her shoulders. "It's okay," she said softly in her ear. "It's only Dr. Hollinger."

"Cecelia, I completely understand why you would feel so uncomfortable with me." Derek sat down in his chair. "I look in the mirror and I'm uncomfortable with myself."

"Why are you like this?" Cecelia asked, quickly marking the sign of the cross.

"I don't know." Derek gripped the arms of his chair. "I haven't been able to figure it out yet."

Cecelia's voice softened. "How did it happen?"

Derek rubbed his chin, trying to use the right words. "There is an old shaman woman who says that she was trying to reconnect my soul. Somehow things went wrong when I ran away from her."

Cecilia's eyes widened. "That's not good."

Kendal eased her into one of the chairs that sat in front of the desk.

"No, it's not," Derek agreed, shaking his head.

"What are you going to do?" She looked across the desk at him with concern on her face.

"I am still trying to work that out."

"Where is the shaman woman?" Cecilia sat stiff as a board.

"She's very sick in a hospital right now," Derek admitted. "I don't know if she is going to live."

"She must live. She cannot leave you like this!" Her eyes welled up.

"I agree." Derek stood up. "Cecelia, I have a favor to ask of you."

"Yes, Dr. Hollinger." There was sympathy in her expression.

"I have a young woman coming in tomorrow who works for a patient of mine." He kept his voice soft, looking down at his hands. "We believe she may be in some sort of trouble." He looked Cecelia in the eyes. "But we are not sure because she only speaks Spanish. She has not really talked to us. We would like you to come back tomorrow and translate for us. I will pay you for your trouble."

"Of course, Dr. Hollinger, I can do this." She looked over at Kendal.

Derek swung his chair around and stepped out from behind his desk. Cecelia jumped up and took a step back. Kendal laid a reassuring hand on her arm.

"Thank you, I really appreciate it." Derek took a step back. "Kendal will work with you to see if there is anything we can do to assist this young woman."

"Okay, Dr. Hollinger." Cecelia slowly backed out the door, not taking her eyes off him.

Kendal held Cecelia gently by the arm. "Let me walk you down to your car."

Derek sat at his desk writing in Ami Soo's chart. When Kendal returned, he looked up, laid down his pen, and smiled. "Well, I think that went well," he said.

Kendal slipped down into one of the chairs, her arms stretched out on the armrests. "I'm glad I went down to her car; she was still jumpy." She scratched her neck. "I think if I would have let her go alone, she might not have come back tomorrow."

"She's still pretty spooked, huh?" He leaned back in his chair.

"Uh, yeah, wouldn't you be?" Kendal stared at his face. It was covered in intricate tattoos, yet she still found herself drawn to him. She remembered how she felt when she first saw Derek and understood the visceral shock Cecelia was feeling, especially after what happened to her in the graveyard when she was a kid.

"So, what do you think the odds are of her showing up tomorrow?" Derek asked.

Kendal shrugged. His deep blue eyes locked with hers, seeming to penetrate her soul. She looked away. "Your guess is as good as mine."

Chapter 20

Derek and Kendal arrived at the office to find Ami Soo and Marie waiting in the hall.

"You're early," Derek said as he approached the two young women.

"I am so excited," Ami Soo said. "Look at my face!"

"I can see you are doing very well."

"It's almost gone. I can't believe it." Ami Soo grinned.

"Today should complete the procedure," Derek said as Kendal unlocked the office door. "Have a seat, let us turn on some lights and we'll be right with you."

"Okay." Ami Soo said, gesturing for Marie to sit next to her on the couch.

Kendal walked through the office turning on lights, while Derek went straight back to his office. She called the young women back to an exam room, telling Ami Soo she would return shortly and closing the door.

"Do you think Cecelia is going to show up?" Kendal asked Derek in a low voice.

Just at that moment, the chime at the front door rang.

"Well, that answers my question," Kendal said with a tight smile. "Be right back."

She ran down the hall and found Cecelia standing at the front door, her purse clutched to her chest.

"Good morning, Cecelia, how are you this morning?"

"Tired. I didn't sleep very well."

"Oh no. Why not?"

"Because I dreamed of that man, *El Diablo*, I keep having the nightmares." She wrung her hands together. "He scares me."

"Oh, Cecelia, I am so sorry. We didn't mean to bring up childhood nightmares."

"This is why I didn't want to see the doctor."

"Well, the young lady is here. Have a seat and let's take care of this and then you can go. Okay?"

"Yes, *sí*, please."

Kendal went back to the room where Ami Soo sat ready to go. "Okay, let's get this last one done." Kendal smiled and took Ami Soo's arm to lead her down the hall to the laser room.

Derek entered. "This one is not going to take as long," he explained. "We have done most of the major work. This is just going to be finishing things up."

"Okay, wonderful," Ami Soo said happily.

Kendal left the room immediately and went back out to the waiting area, motioning for Cecelia to follow her to the exam room. She stepped inside with Cecelia close behind. "This is her," she said, closing the door and gesturing to Marie, who eyed them both warily. "We only have a few minutes so let's find out what we can. Ask her where she comes from."

"*¿De donde eres?*" Cecelia asked. She sat down in the chair next to the young woman, then translated her response. "She is from a very small village in Colombia. It sounds like maybe in the jungle. It's hard to understand, this is not the same Spanish that I speak."

"Ask her where her parents are," Kendal said.

"*¿Donde estan tus padres?* . . . I think she says that they are with the spirits."

"Okay, ask her how she came to be with these people."

"*¿Por que estas con estas personas?*" Cecilia cocked her head, listening. "They took her away from her village."

"Were you looking for work?" Kendal asked.

"*¿Estabas buscando trabajo?*" Cecilia shook her head. "No, she didn't want to come here."

"So, they came to your village and took you?" Kendal asked.

"*¿Te llevaron?* Yes, and some other people," Cecilia answered.

"Okay." Kendal's cheeks flushed with anger. "And have you told anyone that they had taken you?"

"*¿Has dicho a nadie?*"

Marie looked terrified. Cecilia gave her an encouraging smile and spoke a few firm words in Spanish. After a moment, Marie hesitantly answered.

"No," Cecilia told Kendal. "I think they drugged her, and she has not been able to talk to anyone. They said if she told anyone, they would kill her grandmother."

Kendal and Cecilia exchanged a worried look.

"Where do you stay?" Kendal asked gently. "At the house?"

"*¿Donde te quedas? En la casa?* Yes, with Ami Soo. But they said they have a man that will be coming to get her soon."

"Okay, try to make sure you come back with Ami Soo on her next visit, okay?"

"*Tratar de volver.* Okay, *gracias.*"

They walked out and closed the door, leaving Marie in the room.

Kendal walked Cecelia to the door. "Thank you, Cecelia. Would you be able to help one more time if I need you?"

"Yes. *Sí.*" She shook her head. "This is so sad. I feel so bad for this poor girl."

"Okay. I will be in touch." Kendal said with a hug.

Kendal turned and went back into the laser room where Ami Soo was off the table talking to Derek.

"All finished." Derek said with a smile.

"Wonderful," Kendal said with a forced smile. "Let's get you back to your room and cleaned up so you can go home. We are going to need to make one more follow-up appointment to make sure everything has healed properly. So, let's not forget to take care of that before you leave." She shot a quick glance back at Derek as they left the room.

"So, you are not going to believe what I found out!" Kendal said, rushing back into Derek's office after ushering Ami Soo and Marie out.

"What did you find out?" He took a swig from his coffee cup.

"They kidnapped her from her village, can you believe that?"

"Wow, no, I wasn't expecting that." He set the cup down.

"They went to her village promising the people work and then it sounds like they basically kidnapped them. Well, at least they kidnapped *her*, and there is a man coming for her soon. We must help her."

"When is Ami Soo's next appointment?"

"Tomorrow. I figured we had better bring her right back in."

"That was a great move, but how are we going to get Marie away from them?"

"The same way you were going to get Tyler's brother away from them, right? While you are taking care of Ami Soo, I will make arrangements for Marie to escape."

Derek gazed at her with admiration. "Darn, you are smart *and* beautiful."

"Isn't that why you love me?" Kendal said with a wink.

He grinned. "Okay. I think I am going to need Terry to back us up on this one." Derek pulled his cellphone out of his pocket. "I had better let him know what is going on. On second thought, I had better give Father Mike a call first. I'm sure he can find a place for her to stay once we get her away from these people. I need to talk to him to figure out how we are going to handle this."

Scrolling for the number on his phone, he pushed the button, put it on speaker, and set it on his desk. But before he could explain his current dilemma, Derek was greeted with unexpected and unwelcome news.

"I'm sorry, Derek, the old shaman woman, she passed away this morning." Father Mike said solemnly.

Derek's heart dropped when he heard the news. The old shaman woman, a figure who had been a looming presence in his quest for answers as to why he was covered in tattoos, had passed away. He may not have known her personally, but he had connected with her, her wrinkled face and powerful brown eyes always commanding respect.

Derek stood at the edge of his desk, feeling a sense of loss that he couldn't quite explain. Perhaps it was the feeling of losing a link to the answers he so desperately needed, or maybe it was the realization that death was a constant force, one that could snatch anyone at any time. Just as it had to his grandmother.

The old shaman woman may have been a stranger to him, but in a way, she was a part of him. And with her passing, that part felt lost and hollow.

"Now what am I supposed to do?" He shot a distressed look up at Kendal. "She said that once I found her granddaughter that she would do something for me, and I'm sure she meant she was going to take these tattoos off."

"She never had the power to do that." Father Mike sounded so certain.

"Sure she did. She put them here." Derek looked down at his ink-covered hand.

"She may have been instrumental in some way using her dark power to manifest these markings, but she never had the ultimate power unless you were willing to give it to her."

"Why do you keep saying that?" He shook his head in frustration.

"I am telling you that the only thing that can truly save you and cleanse your soul is the awesome power of God. That's it. There is no one else. The devil can tell you lies, put tattoos on your body, give you cancer and all kinds of diseases. But when you wash yourself clean with the blood of Jesus Christ, the devil can't touch you. You must believe and have faith, and the only way you are going to see the glory of the Lord move is for you to start acting in faith. In the bible, when Daniel was going to be thrown into the furnace, he still refused to bow down before King Nebuchadnezzar. He stood in resistance in faith. As long as you are looking elsewhere and are willing to bow down to another source, you are doomed."

"Then what am I supposed to do now? *She said* that she would find the missing piece of my soul."

"Isaiah 55 says, '*Incline your ear and come to me; hear that your soul may live; and I will make with you an everlasting covenant.*' God will show you. Have faith. When he shows you what to do, make sure you act upon it. Don't make excuses, just do it."

"Okay. But what can *I do*? How will I know?"

"Well, you can continue to live your life only *depending on yourself*. How's that been working for you?"

"Not so good."

"So, why don't you give God a chance? *It shall be health to thy navel and marrow to thy bones.* That means that he will become the center of your life. Seek him out. Listen to him."

"Okay, okay, Father. I think I'm starting to get the picture."

"Good. Where's Kendal?"

"She's here."

"How are things going with the two of you?"

"We're trying to work it out."

"She needs to be in the same place in her spiritual development. If you continue to grow in your faith and she doesn't, you will grow apart. Keep that in mind, okay?"

Kendal nodded with a thin smile.

"Yes, I understand," Derek said, locking eyes with Kendal. "Thank you. Listen, Father, the reason I called is we have a young girl who might have been kidnapped, it appears to be human trafficking, and we need a place to send her once we remove her from her captors."

"Of course, this is a tremendous problem that has grown like a cancer in our country. Anything I can do to help."

"Well, we will probably bring her down to San Diego to you tomorrow. I don't want her anywhere near here once we remove her from the situation."

"Okay, no problem."

"I'm going to have a friend of mine, Cecelia, bring her over to you. She speaks Spanish and has been able to converse on a limited basis with the young girl."

"No problem," Father Mike repeated. "I will speak with you again tomorrow. Remember, '*Trust in the Lord with all thine heart; and lean not unto thine own understanding. In all thy ways acknowledge him, and he shall direct thy paths.*'"

Derek hung up, shoulders slumped. He put his head in his hands. Kendal walked around the desk, sat down on his lap, and put her arms around his shoulders.

"I'm so sorry." She could feel the muscles in his body slacken. The physical connection made her want to express her willingness to forgive.

"I'm just sick. I don't know what I am going to do now." He buried his head in her shoulder.

She stroked his head. "Have faith. That's what Father Mike was telling us to do, right?"

"Yes," he murmured.

"Okay. Well, then, don't get yourself all worked up and thinking the worst. Let's pray."

"What?" He looked up into her face.

Kendal looked him directly in the eyes. "You know, let's pray."

"I . . . I'm not sure how," Derek admitted.

She reached for one of his hands. "Dear Father, we thank you for being here for us. Please give Derek the answers he is looking for. Dear Lord, whatever is not for your glory in his body, we ask for it to be removed, please give him peace and resolution, and complete restoration. Lord, please come into his heart and guide him. Thank you. Amen."

"Thank you, Kendal." Expressing gratitude had been the last thing on his mind, but somehow, he felt significantly better. He kissed the top of her hand.

"Good." She kissed his forehead, then slowly stood. She felt the unease of being between a rock and a hard spot. She knew her support was necessary, but she still wasn't ready to recommit—and now she was in deeper than ever. At what personal cost?

Chapter 21

Derek met Terry Ford at his bar. The neon sign out front flashed "The Old Ford Bar," with his old Ford truck depicted at the bottom, while they sat inside the dimly lit bar and discussed the strange situation of Ami Soo. Derek had called in his friend for backup after discovering that Ami Soo was ZhiZhu's sister.

"It's a volatile situation," Derek said. When ZhiZhu finds out, I don't know how he is going to react. And to make matters worse, we need an escape plan for Marie."

Terry remembered watching Derek give Ami Soo his business card before he left. Little did either one of them know at the time that Ami Soo was ZhiZhu's sister.

Derek knew he could depend on Terry's military expertise. Terry set to work to devise the plan.

When the front door chimed the next day, Kendal greeted Ami Soo and Marie, then escorted them back to the exam room. Shortly thereafter, Cecelia came in, and Kendal put her in the room next door.

Derek determined after examining Ami Soo's face that she needed one more quick laser treatment. They walked to the end of the hall and entered the laser room.

Kendal motioned for Cecelia to follow her silently. They entered the exam room, where Marie sat with her head hanging and a look of blank despair.

"Marie," Kendal said quietly.

Her head came up lethargically.

"Marie, are you okay?"

She did not speak. Her pupils looked dilated.

Kendal walked over and checked her pulse. "I think they've drugged her."

"Oh, no," Cecelia gasped.

"Come on, I'll help you walk her down to the car. We must hurry."

They both grabbed an arm; Marie was slow and heavy.

"Come on, Marie, you must walk quickly," Kendal urged. "We need to go to the car. Come on, we are going to go home now. Tell her, Cecilia."

"*Sí, sí, volver a casa. Prisa,*" Cecelia encouraged.

Marie stumbled as they tried to quicken her pace. Kendal decided to take the elevator since the stairs would be impossible. When they reached the ground floor, she had Cecelia stay in the elevator as she stepped out to look around. "Where's your car?"

Cecelia pointed.

"Go get it and drive over here."

Kendal stood holding the door with one hand and Marie with the other for what seemed like an eternity. The elevator open door alarm started to go off. The car finally drove up with Cecelia at the wheel. Kendal let the doors close, silencing the alarm. She helped Marie into the passenger side.

"Straight to the hospital; do not stop for anyone. Go, go. Call me when you get to San Diego."

"*Sí. Sí.* I will call you," Cecelia promised.

Marie's head rolled back against the seat.

"Bye, go." Kendal waved her off.

The little car sped away. Kendal pushed the elevator button as she looked around the parking lot. Not seeing anyone, she stepped inside. Just as the door closed, she glimpsed a familiar face. Kendal's heart pounded as the car began to ascend. She bolted out of the elevator on the office floor and ran down the hall. Derek was walking Ami Soo back to the exam room.

"May I speak to you please?" she said, trying to appear calm.

"Sure, let me just take Ami Soo back to the exam room."

"Here, let's have her wait over here for a second," Kendal said cheerfully.

She grabbed a startled Ami Soo by the arm, pushed her into a room, and closed the door.

"They know," Kendal hissed. "He saw me, he saw us!"

"They know what?" Derek frowned.

"That we took the girl. He saw me!"

"Who saw you?"

"Angel." Kendal paused to draw a deep breath. "When I was getting on the elevator, he was watching me."

"Okay," Derek said firmly. "We have Terry as our backup. He's the wild card in my pocket. Let's see what is going to happen when ZhiZhu finds out. Let me go talk to Ami Soo."

Derek and Kendal entered the room where Ami Soo sat waiting. She jumped up from her seat with furrowed brows.

"What's going on? Is there a problem?"

"There might be, but not with you," Derek replied.

She stepped forward. "Why, what do you mean?"

"Marie is gone," Derek stated bluntly.

Her eyes widened. "What do you mean?"

"Well, we had someone give her a ride out of town." He watched her reaction closely.

Ami Soo's face screwed up in confusion. "Why would you do that?"

"We believe that she was taken from her village against her will and she wants to go back home."

"No." Ami Soo shook her head. "She came here for work and my brother is helping her."

"Do you speak Spanish?" Kendal asked.

"No," she admitted.

"Well, we have a woman that does and she has told us this information."

"Well, then, she is lying to you!" Her face burned red. Amo Soo looked like she was going to cry.

"It doesn't matter. She is underage, and she must be returned to her family."

"My brother is going to be very upset." She blinked back tears. "There is a man who is supposed to pick her up today for a job."

"Okay, well you can have your brother call me," Derek said.

"Oh, I'm sure he is going to do more than call you." She pushed past the pair and stormed out of the room.

"So much for *good will*," Kendal said with a weak smile.

Derek and Kendal sat in his office waiting for the call. The first to come in was from Terry.

"They just left the house, probably on their way to you. We will stay close. I have two men coming up to your office right now."

"Thanks, Terry." Derek set his cellphone on the desk.

They heard the chime of the reception area bell. Derek motioned for Kendal to stay back as he walked slowly out to the lobby. He returned with two of Terry's men.

"I think we are going to split up. One of us in the front of the office and the other in the back in case things get a little rough," one of the men said.

Derek nodded. "That works for me."

"If they're packing heat and pull guns and we have to step in, just hit the deck or jump behind something."

Derek's eyes widened. "Sure, okay." He looked at Kendal.

"Don't try to do anything," the man reiterated firmly. "We don't want anyone to get hurt. Let's see if we can talk our way out of this."

"Okay, understood." Derek winced.

The two men separated and took their positions nearby while Derek and Kendal sat back down in the office.

"Sorry, I got you into this mess." Derek looked grim.

"Don't say that. I insisted, remember?" Kendal's face softened. "I wanted to help, to make sure they knew you weren't doing anything unsavory with his sister. Plus, it was my idea to save this girl. No one should be sorry except ZhiZhu. He's the one taking young girls away from their homes and selling them into slavery—"

She cut off as a loud explosive noise came from the front office. Derek jumped up from his seat. Another blast came, when he heard the marble table in the waiting room go flying against the wall. "Tatman, where are you?" ZhiZhu's deep voice broke the silence.

Derek motioned for Kendal to stay put. He cautiously stepped out from his office. One of Terry's men stood concealed in a doorway, gun ready with the barrel pointed up. He put a finger to his lips as Derek walked slowly down the hall to the front, where ZhiZhu stood glowering with two thugs.

Terry's other man was hiding behind the low wall on the other side of the reception desk. Derek made a concerted effort not to look in his direction so as not to give his presence away.

Meanwhile, Kendal inched her way along the corridor and slipped into an empty exam room.

"Where's my girl?" ZhiZhu growled.

"She's not here," Derek answered calmly.

"Where have you taken her?" He clenched his fists.

"I can't tell you because to tell you the truth, I really don't know."

"Tatman," he clenched his teeth, "you have been a pain in my ass." He reached behind his back and pulled out a gun. "First you welch on our fight deal, and now you steal one of my girls."

Derek put both his hands out front where they could be seen. "What do you think about your sister's new face?"

ZhiZhu's eyes narrowed. "What does that have to do with anything?"

"Because I did it," Derek said flatly.

He cocked his head back. "You removed the mark from her face?"

"Yes. I did."

ZhiZhu's mouth twisted. "Why?"

"Because I knew that she suffered having it there, and I want her to have a better life."

"What did she promise you in return? The girl?" ZhiZhu raised the gun.

Derek shook his head, putting up one hand. "No, no nothing like that."

ZhiZhu waved the gun. "Then why are you telling me this?"

"Because, ZhiZhu, I never would have known about the girl if I had not agreed to take the mark off of your sister's face out of kindness."

"We don't need your kindness." He tightened his grip on the gun. "We need the girl!"

Derek raised both hands higher. "Look, ZhiZhu, your sister has her life back. Let's call it even."

His body tensed. "You don't get to decide what is even." He jabbed the gun in Derek's direction.

"Okay, what do you consider even?"

"Give me the girl back and I'll forget the whole thing since you took care of my sister."

"That's not going to happen."

"Then we are going to take you out and kill you," ZhiZhu snarled, twisting the gun sideways.

Kendal let out an audible gasp.

"Ah, who do we have here?" ZhiZhu called. "Come out!"

Kendal covered her mouth. Across the hall, Terry's man shook his head *no*.

"Come out here, or I'll pop him in the head right now!"

Kendal slowly stepped out from the exam room.

"She's just an employee," Derek said tightly, his chest tightening with real fear now.

Eyes wide, Kendal's head snapped in Derek's direction, hurt by the words even though she knew he was only trying to protect her. With her attention drawn to Derek, ZhiZhu stepped forward, grabbing her by the neck. He put his face close to hers. "She's a little old, but she will have to do," ZhiZhu said, pushing her over to one of his men.

"She's not leaving here." A low guttural sound came from Derek's throat as he lunged for the gun.

Then, a pop. Kendal hit the ground. Terry's men stepped out and began to fire their weapons at the two men, who returned fire. ZhiZhu and Derek continued to struggle as the gun battle raged around them. One of Terry's men took a bullet to the shoulder but continued to fire.

When the two men behind Kendal dropped to the floor, she jumped up and landed a roundhouse kick to the side of ZhiZhu's head. Derek fell with him. Jumping up quickly to regain his balance, he was shocked to see ZhiZhu lying on the ground out cold.

"Wow," Derek exclaimed, looking over at Kendal.

"I know ... practice pays off." She rushed over to Terry's injured man, grabbing a towel off the counter and pressed it to the wound. She looked up at Derek. "What did you mean *just an employee*?"

Before he could explain, in through the door came Terry and two police officers.

"When my guys called to tell me ZhiZhu and his men had arrived, I called the police." Terry chomped hard on his cigar.

"That was a good call, but they are little late," Derek said wryly, glancing at Kendal. "Thank God I had my bodyguard here."

In came the paramedics, in their blue uniforms. The police, already on the scene, pointed to where Kendal was helping compress the shoulder wound of the victim. She stepped aside to let them do their job, her heart still racing from adrenaline.

Derek approached her, his own body trembling with the aftermath of the chaos. He pulled her into his arms, holding her tight as he buried his face in her hair. The warmth of her body and the scent of her shampoo filled his senses, and he felt a rush of gratitude for her quick thinking and bravery. With a grateful smile, he kissed the top of her head and held her close, knowing that without her, the outcome could have been much worse.

As the paramedics worked on the victim, Derek couldn't help but replay the events in his mind. He knew that Kendal had put herself in harm's way to help him, and he couldn't be more proud of her. In that moment, he felt a deep appreciation for her and the love that they shared, and he vowed to never take her for granted again.

Derek looked at Kendal under his arm, then kissed her on the forehead.

Terry smiled, "Kendal did this?"

"Yeah, she saved my life." He gave her a squeeze.

After being questioned by the police, Kendal asked Terry, "How are ZhiZhu's men doing?"

"Looks like one didn't make it, but the other one should be okay. ZhiZhu is going to have a nasty concussion. We found out that he's been doing quite a bit of business on his own—he seems to have gone rogue. So I don't think anyone is going to come to his defense. In fact, I think he's going to be in big-time trouble for drawing attention to the organization." Terry snickered.

"Do you think this is going to be the end of it?" Derek asked.

"For you, yeah. I don't think you are going to have any more trouble from ZhiZhu. He's facing a lot of charges, including attempted murder and human trafficking. He's going to jail for a very long time—if he makes it that far."

"What do you mean?" Kendal asked.

"Well, when you cross the mafia, they don't let you live very long."

"Oh." She breathed out audibly.

"Listen. Come by the shop soon." He adjusted his cap. "Okay?"

"Terry, thanks again for all your help. Tell your guys thank-you, and if any of you or your families need anything, I am here for you." Derek shook his hand.

"That's what it's all about." Terry saluted.

Chapter 22

When he reached the hospital, Father Mike was just in time to see Cecelia pull up at the emergency room entrance. Cecelia immediately spotted Father Mike, a minister in his late forties, with a kind face and a gentle demeanor.

He could see the panic and desperation etched on her face. They quickly escorted a disoriented Marie through the glass doors. The emergency room buzzed with activity. Father Mike was able to flag down a nurse, who admitted Marie immediately. Cecilia began to explain the story to him. How she was Dr. Hollinger's housekeeper and she had not seen him for a while because of the tattoos, but that she had received a call a couple days previous asking for help with this young woman.

That's when it occurred to Father Mike that this might be the very girl that the old shaman woman had been looking for. He thought of the old woman, her desperate plea for Derek to find the granddaughter. The sadness in her eyes when she had been brought to the hospital near death and realized that her search had been in vain. The old woman now lay in the morgue waiting for her body to be claimed.

Father Mike felt a wave of sadness and anger wash over him as Cecelia told him the young girl's story. He listened as she described the tragedy of Marie's kidnapping, her struggles during captivity, and the cruel deception of telling people she was there for work but in reality was being trafficked for nefarious reasons. He felt a strong responsibility to make sure that Marie was safe. He prayed that these demons would be brought to justice.

After a couple of hours on intravenous fluids, Marie became alert and was able to talk. Father Mike suggested to Cecelia that she ask Marie to explain what had happened to her.

"They locked me in the room next to Ami Soo," Marie explained in Spanish. "The window had been nailed shut and my door locked. When Ami Soo went to bed, I was able to loosen the nail with a finger-nail file that I grabbed from the bathroom. I climbed out my bedroom window. But before I could make it to the street, one of ZhiZhu's men caught me and took me back into the house. That is when ZhiZhu drugged me so that I wouldn't try to escape again."

Father Mike and Cecelia couldn't help but admire her courage. Marie continued to tell her story, her voice becoming more urgent and passionate as she went on. She described a vision she'd had and her powerful feeling when she saw her grandmother in the vision and the determination it had given her to take control of her own destiny.

"My grandmother came to me in a vision," she said, her eyes wide with amazement. "She said she was coming to rescue me. I didn't understand it at first, but then I realized what it meant. That's when I decided I had to do something to save myself."

Father Mike listened as Cecelia translated, captivated by Marie's narrative and her strength in the face of adversity. By the time Marie had finished, they were filled with admiration for the young woman.

Father Mike asked Marie if she would come to look at an old woman who had recently passed away. It was hard to tell how much of the translation she understood, but she seemed more than willing to follow. Father Mike, Cecelia, and Marie arrived downstairs in the basement morgue to find the body had already been placed out for viewing, shrouded in a white sheet.

Marie's expression was one of confusion and surprise, having thought she was being led to meet someone. Miscommunication between dialects. She gasped as Father Mike pulled back the linen sheet and exposed her grandmother's face.

Immediately, they could see that Marie had the same sharp features as her grandmother, but with tears tumbling down her face. Cecelia felt a chill go through her as she looked at the still figure lying on the cold steel table. She had never seen a dead person before except that day in the graveyard as a child.

Father Mike looked sadly at the body for a few moments before turning toward Marie. He laid a gentle hand on her shoulder and spoke quietly, gesturing to the body. "Is this her? Is this your grandmother?"

Cecelia repeated the question in Spanish.

The sight of her grandmother, still but peaceful, drained the color from Marie's cheeks, and she took another deep breath before she began to speak. Marie nodded with big, brown tear-filled eyes.

"*Sí, sí, mi abuela.*" Marie mumbled something else.

"Marie says that she died because *of her*," Cecelia translated.

"Tell her it's not because of her, it's because of ZhiZhu."

Father Mike explained that the old woman had recently passed away from a virus. She had become very sick and weak and had fallen and hit her head, compounding the problem. He told Marie that he believed her grandmother was in California searching for her. She had been trying to elicit help through her shaman powers. He had wanted

Marie to come and see her to confirm that this truly was her grand-mother.

"Do you understand what I am saying?" Father Mike asked.

Cecelia translated. Marie nodded hesitantly, though it was hard to tell how much of the translation she really understood. Her eyes were wide with fear she stepped toward the body. Yet as she reached out to touch the cold, ashen skin of the old woman, peace washed over her face. She closed her eyes.

Father Mike gave a thin smile at the sad reunion. "We are all part of something much bigger than ourselves," he said. "Your grandmother is now at peace, she obviously loved you very much to come on such a long and perilous trip to rescue you."

Marie nodded slowly, her gaze fixed on the body before her. She took a deep breath and bowed her head. Father Mike assumed she was saying a silent prayer for the old woman.

"Let's give her a couple minutes," Father Mike suggested.

Cecelia and Father Mike walked out of the room.

"Father Mike, why does Dr. Hollinger have all the tattoos on him? Isn't this the work of the devil?" she asked.

Father Mike paused for a moment, considering her words. He had had a few conversations with Dr. Hollinger, and he was not a fan of the man's lifestyle. But he had no evidence to suggest that the tattoos were of a diabolical nature.

"I believe whatever is not the work of God is the work of the devil or of man," he said slowly. "I'm not sure which one this is. But I can assure you, he is not going to find salvation until he finds his way with God."

"*Sí*, I understand, gracias."

"Marie may be able to help us understand what was going on with her grandmother. Derek, Dr. Hollinger, believes that the old woman may be a shaman and linked to a curse that may have facilitated the appearance of his tattoo tapestry. Let's see how she is doing."

The morgue was dark and quiet, illuminated only by intermittently flickering fluorescent lights. They had left Marie standing in the center of the room, her small body framed by a gurney and a narrow table.

Now, Father Mike and Cecelia pushed open the morgue doors to find the room empty.

Chapter 23

Derek arrived back at the penthouse just in time to catch Tyler leaving with his duffel bag slung over one shoulder.

"Where are you going?" he asked.

Head hung low, Tyler replied, "I don't know yet."

"Come back in—let's talk for a minute." Derek closed the door. "We put ZhiZhu in jail today."

"Really? Oh wow, that is great news." Tyler gave a little smile. "Did you do that?"

"It's a pretty long story but in a nutshell, he came to see me at my office today. Terry had his men waiting for him. It was Kendal who actually took him down when she landed a kick to the head when he pulled a gun on us and tried to kidnap her. The police took him into custody. Yeah, so I don't think he's going to be dealing drugs for a while."

"That's crazy. I am really sorry I have caused you all this trouble."

"You didn't cause me trouble. ZhiZhu needed to be put away." Derek stuck his hands in his back pockets. "Listen, I've been thinking about this, and I have an offer to make."

"Really? An offer for me?" Tyler set his bag on the floor.

"Yes. I want you to stay here and go back to school. I will pay for your school and mentor you. What do you think about that?"

"I don't know." His brow furrowed. "It sounds a little too good to be true."

"Yeah, I know. But here's the deal." Derek put his hands behind his back and started to pace. "When I was a kid, there was a man that stepped up to take care of me. He mentored me, he paid for my schooling, and even brought me into his business and that is how I ended up here."

Tyler cocked his head, his expression one of mild disbelief. "Wow . . . okay."

"What I would like to do is pay it forward—do the same for you. I'm not doing anything for you that hasn't already been done for me." Derek stopped pacing and swallowed hard. "You can live here until you finish school. I will tutor you and pay for all your expenses. But you must be serious about getting your degree, that's all I ask." He waved his hand. "In whatever profession you decide you would like to pursue."

Tyler nodded. He drew a breath and explained that he'd pondered what to do with his life ever since he was a child. He'd finally settled on becoming an academic, and his dreams of achieving greatness were evident in his dedication to the tradition of his magical tattoos. Growing up as a Marine's son had exposed him to both Eastern and Western cultures, and his recent studies in Thailand had focused on the healing techniques originating from ancient practices.

"I would love to study medicine," Tyler said, pressing his palms together. "I would like to join the Eastern and Western traditions."

"I can help you do that." Derek smiled.

"I don't know what to say." His eyes welled.

"Just say yes." Derek laughed.

"Yes, of course. Thank you."

The two men hugged. The idea was ambitious, but Derek could see that Tyler was determined to make it a reality. With his newfound passion in mind, Tyler would set off on his journey, hoping to find the knowledge that would bring his dreams to life. He was determined to learn all he could about medicine, and Derek was certain that if he worked hard enough, he could make his dreams a reality.

Derek patted him on the back and released him from the hug, "Okay, then go put your stuff back in your room."

"I don't understand, what do you mean *gone*?" Derek asked Father Mike as he stood in the foyer outside his penthouse door.

"I mean Cecelia and I were standing outside the door talking one minute and the next they were gone. Both the old woman's body and Marie."

"How could that happen?" Derek braced a hand on the wall to steady himself.

"I don't know. We were standing in front of the only set of doors. There are no other doors. It's a morgue, for goodness' sake."

"What's the explanation then? You're a man of God, what does God say?"

"It's something supernatural," Father Mike admitted with a shrug. "Something beyond our reality."

It had kept him up all night, this unexplainable event. He'd harkened back to his college days, recalling what he had learned in physics class. He still had his old textbook and he had flipped through it, searching for answers.

"According to science," Father Mike explained, "there are seven fundamental qualities or dimensions of the physical world: mass, length, time, temperature, electric current, luminous intensity, and amount of substance. But I couldn't make sense of how these concepts could possibly explain the shaman woman's sudden disappearance, or that of her granddaughter as well.

"However, the seventh dimension offers endless possibilities to explore different universes," he said, idly scratching the back of his head while his brow knit in thought, "including the idea of parallel universes."

Derek's eyes widened a little. "You're not joking."

"Not in the least. A being existing in the seventh dimension may have the ability to observe and engage with all lower dimensions in ways that are beyond our current understanding." Father Mike gave a slow exhale. "However, this is purely theoretical and falls within the realm of science fiction, in my opinion."

Derek sadly shook his head while Father Mike carried on talking.

"After reading that, I took some time to meditate and pray. I searched my Bible for guidance, and this is the spiritual answer that I found. The Bible speaks of seven dimensions in understanding the physical world, represented by the sevenfold ministry of the Spirit. These include the Spirit of the Lord and the Spirits of wisdom, understanding, counsel, might, knowledge, and fear of the Lord, all of which are before the throne of God.

"Each dimension is essential in our spiritual journey to comprehend the world around us. I can only surrender myself to this situation and have faith that God will guide us toward the answers we need."

"So what do you suggest I do now?" Derek wondered.

Father Mike smiled. "The same advice I've been giving all along. Trust in the Lord. If it's not of the Kingdom of God, then it's of the devil or of man, and I'll tell you right now, this is not of the Kingdom of God, I promise you."

"I still feel very confused as to how all of this could happen. How it is all connected. What should I do next?" He stepped into the penthouse. "Come in, sorry, come inside."

Father Mike entered the elegant foyer. "I suggest you pray for your answer."

"I've done that." Derek fell back into a chair.

"Then have faith that it will come."

"Okay, but when?"

"I can't tell you." He stood in front of Derek, who sat with his head in his hands.

"Thank you, Father." Derek looked up. "I really appreciate your coming here to tell me."

"I felt I needed to talk to you in person because this is not something that happens every day and it's hard to explain . . ." Father Mike trailed off with a smile. "I see Tyler out on the deck. How is he doing?"

Derek looked in the direction of the kitchen window. "I've offered him to stay here with me and go back to school."

"Bless you." He made the sign of the cross.

"Someone once had the heart to take me in. The least I can do is give him a helping hand. You know—pay it forward."

"This is going to go a long way with your healing process and for your deliverance." Father Mike put a hand on his shoulder.

"Really? You think so? Now that I lost the connection with the old woman after finding her granddaughter?" Derek eyes reflected a tiredness.

"Absolutely. When you give of the heart like this, it makes all the difference in the world. The way you stepped up for this young woman, taking her away from her captors. Cecelia told me how you found the old woman's granddaughter by doing pro-bono work on the criminal's sister. These are all the things a Christian does when he walks the walk of Jesus. 'Thou shalt love the Lord with all thy heart, and with all thy soul, and with all thy mind.' This is the first commandment. And the second is 'Thou shalt love thy neighbor as thyself.' You will be blessed soon with the answers you are seeking. Trust me, God sees your heart."

"Thank you, Father, I sure hope so. I really appreciate you saying that." Derek placed his hands on his knees, then pushed to stand.

"It truly has nothing to do with me and everything to do with you and your spiritual walk. It has gone from being all about you to being about taking care of others." Father Mike started walking toward the front door. "Even though you have this situation going on, you are still reaching out to help people, while you are experiencing your own struggles. God recognizes that. This is what God calls us to do."

"Well, I can only hope." Derek followed him out.

Father Mike turned back to face Derek. "Have faith."

"Okay, have faith," he repeated. "I understand. Thank you."

"How are you and Kendal doing?"

"Better. She seems to be coming around." He gave a small smile. "I don't think she's mad at me anymore."

"Let her know that I asked about her, and if you two ever decide to make a future together, I am here for you."

"Thank you, Father."

"Okay, we will be in touch, right?" Father Mike locked eyes with him.

"Oh, yes, we have a lot of work to do." Derek blinked at Father Mike's persistent request. He stood watching in the doorway until the elevator door closed. Then he went to the kitchen window. Tyler sat in his meditative pose on the balcony, not moving a muscle, as still as a statue.

Derek chuckled and shook his head. "How does he do that?"

Chapter 24

Derek felt a wave of anticipation wash over him as he heard Kendal's voice coming from inside the penthouse. He was sitting on the eastside of the wraparound balcony, sipping his steaming cup of coffee and watching the first signs of morning light filter up over the mountains. The rays flitted to the south across the fog that had settled over the ocean. He had been up for hours, unable to sleep, and had come out to the balcony in an attempt to fill the time.

And then, suddenly, he heard her. His stomach jumped and he quickly set down his mug, feeling his pulse race as he looked up and saw her come around the corner. She wore a white gingham dress that danced around her ankles, and her eyes were bright with excitement.

Smiling softly, she slowly walked toward him, her steps measured and unhurried. Derek rose to his feet, feeling a tingling sensation run through his body as she stopped in front of him. Neither of them spoke, but Derek could feel the electricity, a spark that seemed to ignite the air around them.

Finally, Kendal spoke, her voice low and gentle. "You look like you've been here for hours," she said.

Derek smiled, too overwhelmed to find words. He simply nodded, feeling his heart beat faster and faster. Taking a step closer to him, Kendal smiled and held out her hand.

"Guess what I have?" she said waving a stack of papers in the air.

"Not a clue," Derek answered.

"Five percent of your business," she said with a smile as she dropped into one of the chairs.

Derek stood in front of her, admiring her every move. "You worked hard on those," Derek commented, his voice deep and inviting.

Kendal looked up, her green eyes sparkling with intelligence. She smiled, and Derek felt bathed in a warm, pleasant sensation.

"I don't know why you worked so hard for such a small percentage," Derek teased, looking down at her alluring figure.

"What are you talking about? I think that's a fair deal. I'm not a greedy person, you know that." Her slender fingers expertly waved over the documents laid in front of her. She had scrutinized every detail with the same intensity one would expect from a certified accountant. "It's more about me being paid a reasonable sum for my contribution. I am supporting the partners now, which is a game changer. Plus, it will increase in five years."

"What if I said you could have an even bigger percentage?" he asked as he sat back down in his chair.

"What do you mean?" She arched a brow. "I started out with just three percent and negotiated it up to five. Now you're offering me more?"

"Well, I had a long talk with Father Mike yesterday and it got me thinking. I've come a long way from the person I was just a few months back. With everything we went through lately and after our narrow escape from ZhiZhu trying to kidnap you, it just made me realize how much I really do love you." He swallowed, his mouth suddenly dry. "I mean, if you were to become Mrs. Derek Hollinger, then you would own the controlling stock."

She looked at him from under her fedora with a sly smile. "You know, that is a deal to consider. Wait, have you looked in the mirror lately?"

"Yes, of course—when I took my shower this morning."

"Did you notice how many of your tattoos have disappeared?"

Derek took off his hat and sunglasses, went inside, and gazed into the large mirror on the wall. Staring back at him was his thirty-something face. He had only a couple of tattoos left, both of them small; one on his left temple and one on the right side of his face, barely visible unless you looked closely.

He touched both of them, feeling the bumpy texture of the imagined ink beneath his fingertips. A wave of memories from his past flooded his mind. But the reflection in the mirror only showed a man looking back at him, as if all those experiences had made him a new person.

He didn't know who that person was yet. He only knew that he was standing in the reflection of a new man. He smiled and stepped away from the mirror, taking in the grandeur of the room. He knew he was ready to take on whatever life threw at him next.

Lifting his shirt, he asked, "What about my back?"

"Gone, they're gone. Oh, wait there is still one, the one with the bible."

"What does it say?"

"It just has a bible verse written on it."

"Which one?"

"Psalms 95 and 96. Do you have a bible?"

"Yeah, let me get it."

Derek came back with the bible Father Mike had given him and opened it, flipping the pages. "It says: Psalms 95: *O come let us sing to the Lord; let us make a joyful noise to the rock of our salvation!*" Derek began to choke up as he read out loud. "*Let us come into his presence with thanksgiving: let us make a joyful noise to him with songs of praise! For the Lord is a great God, and a great King above all gods. In his hand are the depths of the earth; the heights of the mountains are his also.*"

Kendal took the bible to read from Psalms 96: "*O sing to the Lord a new song: sing to the Lord all the earth! Sing to the Lord, bless his name; tell of his salvation from day to day. Declare his glory among the nations, his marvelous works among all the peoples! For great is the Lord, and greatly to be praised; he is to be feared above all gods. For all the gods of the peoples are idols; but the Lord made the heavens. Honor and majesty are before him; strength and beauty are in his sanctuary.*"

Kendal stopped reading. "I believe this really does solidify his word in you. What do you think?"

"Yes!" Derek said with excitement. "That is exactly what Father Mike has been telling me. Now, for it to be one of the last tattoos left on me is a clear message as to who I should believe."

Kendal threw her arms around Derek's neck. "So, what were you saying before I interrupted you? What about the percentage of stock?"

"Yes, that. I was asking you if you would like to own a bigger portion of the company."

"And how would that work?"

"You would be Mrs. Derek Hollinger."

"I see."

"How does that sound?"

"Wonderful."

His voice was hoarse with emotion. "I love you, Kendal, and I want you to be my wife."

"I love you too, Derek, and I would love to be your wife." Kendal kissed him, the fedora tumbling from her head.

Derek remembered standing on the shore with her, his heart racing as he watched the sun slowly dip below the horizon. This felt exactly the same. He had dreamed of this moment for what seemed like a lifetime, and now it was finally here. Kendal stood beside him, her hand gently resting on his shoulder.

It had been a long road for Derek, filled with loneliness and isolation. But that all changed when he met Kendal. She showed him a world he never knew existed, a world filled with adventure, love, and possibility. And now, as he stood here with her, he knew that he was truly living.

He turned to her, a soft smile on his lips as he took in her beauty. Just like that day not so long ago when they stood on the beach and her auburn hair danced in the breeze, her green eyes sparkling as she looked back at him. In that moment, he knew he would love her forever and without reserve.

"Thank you," he said, his voice barely above a whisper.

Kendal smiled, understanding the gratitude in his words. She had shown him that life was meant to be lived, not just existed in. And in that realization, they shared a love that was deeper and more profound than either of them could have ever imagined.

They could watch the sun disappear each day and begin a new day together. Signaling the end of their old life and the beginning of their future. They would now walk hand in hand toward their next adventure.

Derek knew that he had found his true purpose in life—to live each moment to the fullest with Kendal by his side.

"Let's call Father Mike and ask him to marry us right away," Derek suggested.

She grinned. "I think that's a great idea."

Father Mike answered the phone immediately.

"We have great news! We're getting married," Derek announced, looking at Kendal's bright smile as he made the proclamation.

"That is wonderful news," Father Mike agreed heartily. "Congratulations."

"We would like you to perform the ceremony," Derek said.

"I would love to—but I can't."

"Oh?" Derek said with surprise as Kendal raised her eyebrows.

"You must go through the rites of becoming a Catholic first," Father Mike explained dryly, "and I don't think you thought that through, did you?"

"No, I hadn't," Derek admitted.

"Well, I'd be honored to bless your union when you do get married, if that is all right with you."

"Yes, Father, I would appreciate that."

"Also, I want you to know that some scripture flashed in my head last night."

"Oh really, what was that?" Derek asked.

The priest's voice was solemn. Derek felt a prickle run down his spine. Of awe and gratitude at what life had given him.

"Whoever sows to please their flesh, from the flesh will reap destruction; whoever sows to please the Spirit, from the Spirit will reap eternal life." (Galatians 8) (6:8)

As they stood on the beach, watching the sun set over the vast expanse of the Pacific Ocean, Derek couldn't help but think of all the moments that led up to this one. The struggles and sacrifices, the moments of doubt and fear, the triumphs and joys. And now, here they were, together, basking in the warmth of the sun and the love that surrounded them.

Kendal's hand was intertwined with his own, her touch bringing him a sense of calm and belonging he had never known before. She had shown him that life was meant to be lived, and with her by his side, he was ready to take on whatever challenges came their way.

He turned to her, taking in her beauty as the soft light of the setting sun illuminated her face. She was his everything, and he couldn't imagine a life without her.

"I love you," he whispered, his voice full of emotion.

Kendal smiled, her eyes shining with love and happiness. "I love you too," she replied, leaning in to kiss him.

As the sun disappeared below the horizon and the sky turned a deep shade of purple, Derek knew that this was just the beginning of their journey together.

And he couldn't wait to see where it would take them next.

About the Author

Writer, speaker, and certified life coach Monica Broussard is passionate about writing fiction that contains elements of fantasy and keeps the reader intrigued about the lead character's motives. She also writes an occasional article for her hometown's magazine, *SeaCliff Living*. She belongs to Toastmasters International and enjoys attending national writers' conferences.

Born in North Carolina on a Marine Corps base, Monica now lives in "Surf City," Huntington Beach, California, with her husband of thirty-eight years. She has enjoyed various occupations over the years, but her favorite job is the one she's doing now—writing.

Her debut novel, *21 Tattoos,* was published by Acorn Publishing in 2023. *The 7th Dimension* is Book 2 in the *21 Tattoos* Series.

If you would like to learn more
about the *21 Tattoos* Series,
please visit Monica Broussard's website
at monicabroussardauthor.com
and sign up to receive email notifications
about updates and future books.